A Gift from
Saint Elmo

By Scott P. Munson

First published by Dog Ear Publishing
4010 W. 86th Street, Ste H
Indianapolis, IN 46268
www.dogearpublishing.net

ISBN: 978-160844-303-1

Printed in the United States of America

PROLOGUE

NEW YORK CITY Firefighter Kyle Murphy could hear his breathing in the facemask of his Scott Pak, a self contained breathing apparatus. He wasn't exactly scared, but he began weighing his options. He was on a fire floor in a five story tenement. A kitchen crystal meth lab had exploded, blowing out through the apartment and into adjacent units. It quickly ran up the interior walls setting apartments above on fire. By the time Murphy's company responded, the upper floors were fully engulfed. During his eight years with the FDNY he had found himself in many difficult situations, some of them life-threatening. From his early days at the training academy, he knew the first rule was, don't panic.

He had a hose line with him but it was useless as it wouldn't charge. The standpipe it was connected to had been clogged with drug paraphernalia quickly stashed in it by junkies when the police were thought to be in the building. This was such a widespread problem for fire-fighters serving the South Bronx that it came to be expected.

A firefighter would never confront a blaze without a charged line and Murphy was no exception. He would crawl below the heat and suffocating smoke while he followed his line back to the standpipe on the lower floor. Once safely away, he would regroup and attack the fire in another way.

Using the hose as a life line he began retracing his route. Along the way he noticed how ripe the conditions were for a flashover, an explosive travel of fire along an enclosed area like a hallway or a small room. The smoke hung thick, still and dark brown waiting to explode into a veritable fireball.

As Murphy approached the stairwell the smoke became so thick he could barely see the hose. He found the stairs and peered through the smoke. Coming from the floor directly below him was the unmistakable soft orange glow of fire. He would have to find another way downstairs.

Still keeping low he followed the hose back to the nozzle. As soon as he felt the familiar shape in his hands, the alarm on his air pack sounded. Murphy was able to grab a few quick breaths before the tank went dry.

Now it was imperative for Murphy to find a way out. Without breathable air he would quickly be overcome by the poisonous smoke.

He left the hose and made his way down the hall. The smoke became less concentrated and Murphy could actually see very faint light coming through a window at the end of the hall. Knowing the approximate layout of the apartment, Murphy was positive he would find a stairwell near it.

There was, but for Murphy it proved to be another dead end. In violation of the New York City Fire Code, the residents on this end of the floor had illegally installed a dead bolt to thwart access to their floor by unwelcomed visitors intent on breaking into their apartments.

Murphy's last option was to go out the window and down the fire escape. He didn't even try to open the window figuring it would be nailed shut. Using the protection of his thick turnout coat he put his elbow through the window several times until it had been smashed to pieces.

The first thing Murphy did after he stepped onto the fire escape was to pull off his facemask and take several deep breaths of fresh air. It was a decision he would pay for dearly.

The immediate infusion of fresh air from the broken window was a magnet for the oxygen starved fire. It raced along the ceiling towards the source of air. It blew out of the window with a force causing Murphy to over-balance. He toppled over the railing from five stories. As he fell, his only thought was how quickly the ground below was rushing up to meet him.

Firefighter Kyle Murphy hit the pavement face first and died instantly.

Ellen Mitchell looked slowly around her office. The sixty four year old senior claims adjuster for Gibral-tar Insurance was doing a mental inventory of how different it would look in three weeks when she retired.

Down would come the framed commendation from the company she worked at for the past forty years. There was also a collection of personal photos that adorned the walls. In her mind's eye, she could see the differences in wall color that would be obvious once the pictures came down.

She never intended to enter the job market, but the death of her husband at an early age left her as the sole support of her children. She took an entry level job as a processing clerk and over the years worked her way up to her present position.

She was looking forward to enjoying a long retire-ment funded by a handsome pension, Social Security Benefits and her life savings. She also promised herself that she would consult her physician about the recurring headache she'd been experiencing over the past few months. She had convinced herself that it had been caused by stress and anxiety but recently the headaches were accompanied by blurred vision.

A complete physical would be the first order of business, or perhaps the second, particularly if she booked the cruise she was thinking of taking.

Ellen was totally unaware she was about to become an actuarial statistic and an insurance claim for her own employer. Over the past few years arteriosclerotic plaque had been building in her carotid arteries. Her thrombosis would be quick and severe.

Noticing her clock said it was quitting time, she tidied her desk, put on her coat, hung her pocketbook strap over her shoulder and left the office.

Walking down the hall toward the elevator another headache hit. She felt that if she could get down to the street into fresh air it would quickly pass.

At the elevator she met up with several coworkers, all with the lobby as their destination. She forced a smile for the ones she recognized and stepped with them into the elevator.

As the door opened at the lobby, Ellen waited for all the passengers to step out. She didn't want anyone to notice the discomfort she was in.

At that moment large portions of Ellen Mitchell's brain began to die. Her world went black and she fell forward hitting the floor half in and half out of the elevator.

In less than twenty four hours she would be one of the nearly one in two victims to die from a stroke.

CHAPTER I

❝.... I'VE NEVER asked for much," said the elderly female voice.

Radio pioneer, Guglielmo Marconi adjusted his earphones trying to connect the pieces of the broken message. There it is again, he thought. Stay with me, dear. Don't break up on me now. For the past few minutes it had been arriving in sporadic bursts. He adjusted the settings of his console in an attempt to clear away the static.

".... my doctor said there isn't much more he can do."

Sitting next to Marconi was electrical genius, Nikola Tesla. Tesla yawned, stretched his arms, then removed his earphones and set them on his console. Both men had been at their stations for two hours and were in need of a break.

Turning his swivel chair to Marconi, Tesla said, "Hey, Marconi. It's break time. You want to grab a cup of coffee?"

Irritated by the interruption, Marconi held up his hand in a silencing gesture.

Seeing Marconi was intent on an incoming message Tesla leaned over and scanned Marconi's monitor looking for the incoming frequency. He saw it and adjusted his own settings to the frequency Marconi was monitoring. The message he heard was faint and broken but the portions he could receive were heartfelt and sincere.

"… time to get my affairs in order."

Tesla reached for his keyboard and typed in an instruction. After he entered it he tapped Marconi on the shoulder to get his attention.

Marconi turned his head and saw Tesla pointing to his screen. On it was a meter measuring incoming passion levels. The meter was numbered from 0 to 100. At the moment, the message they were monitoring was holding steady at 100. Rarely had they seen an unbroken message maintain such a high level of passion. To have a broken one maintain such a high level was unheard of.

Realizing he was monitoring a communication anomaly, Marconi signaled for his supervisor.

Telegraph wizard, Samuel Morse saw Marconi excitedly waving him over. Morse trotted past dozens of other communication technicians, each listening to their own incoming messages. As he arrived at Marconi's station, Marconi said, "Hey, Sam? Plug in and listen to this."

Morse plugged in his earphone jack and began listening intently.

"…but I was wondering if…"

"Damn it," muttered Marconi. "We lost it again."

Morse didn't say anything. He was waiting for any additional parts to the message.

"…heard about this wonderful, heroic man who…"

Suddenly the passion meter began to fall, a sure sign the message was ending.

'…saved me from dying on the Titanic. In the name of The Father, The Son, and The Holy Spirit, Amen."

The men watched as the passion meter dropped to zero. After several moments it was obvious there would be no further message. Morse checked his watch and said, "You two are due for a break. Step into my office for a minute. I want to discuss this with you."

Morse's office was a glass enclosed cubicle giving him full view of the communication center. He was in charge of hundreds of technicians each capable of monitoring thousands of incoming transmissions. He was assigned to the communications bureau upon his arrival in 1872 and was promoted to one of the three supervisory positions in 1905. The other two supervisors were inventors, Alexander Graham Bell and Thomas Edison.

Morse was seated behind his desk while Tesla was seated off to the side. Marconi elected to stand. "Quite strange, indeed." said Morse. "How long have you been monitoring it?"

"Just for the past few days," Marconi replied. "It's very sporadic, but what I can manage to pick up comes in clearly."

"So I heard," said Morse

"What time are the transmissions:" Tesla asked.

"They've all come in at the same time," said Marconi.

"Her bedtime," said Morse.

"Or maybe first thing in the morning," countered Tesla.

"It doesn't matter," said Marconi. "Either way we've got a little old lady trying to get through to us. She obviously wants us to hear her and judging by her passion level, the sooner the better."

"I did hear her say she should get her affairs in order," said Tesla. "Maybe she doesn't have much time left, if you know what I mean."

Morse sat back in his chair and folded his arms across his chest. "I think it deserves special consideration," he said. "I'll give Edgar a call and request a tracer for the next one." He reached for his telephone and dialed the number. When the connection was made Morse said, " This is Mr. Morse over in communications,

I'd like to speak to Mr. Hoover."

While he was waiting for the call to be transferred, Morse winked at Tesla and Marconi and said, "So what if they say the guy liked to wear lingerie? He was still a darn good cop."

Morse suddenly became serious, a signal that former FBI Director, J. Edgar Hoover was on the line. "Hello, Ed? This is Sam. I was wondering if I could have a moment of your time? I've got a situation over here that merits a tracer and I need your department's permission to use it. When might we meet?"

Morse broke into a smile and gave the thumbs up sign. "That'll be fine, Ed. Thank you. We'll see you tomorrow morning."

Morse hung up the phone and said' "Eight AM tomorrow. You guys be ready to state your case to Hoover. If it holds water he said we could have the tracer in place by this time tomorrow."

Each man was excited about the meeting. Tesla's palms were perspiring and he absently wiped them on his pant legs. They had heard a lot about J. Edgar Hoover and were looking forward to being introduced to him.

CHAPTER II

EARLY THE NEXT morning, Morse, Marconi and Tesla were seated at a conference table in J. Edgar Hoover's spacious office. Pitchers of coffee and a large plate of donuts were on the table. Joining Hoover were his seconds in command, lawmen Wyatt Earp and Eliot Ness. It was rumored throughout the security division that Earp's nose was still out of joint after being passed over for promotion in favor of Hoover upon J. Edgar's arrival in 1972. Earp had worked under the then Director of Security, William Barclay "Bat" Masterson since 1929 and felt the job should have been his. After word had filtered up to the CEO a meeting was scheduled to placate any hard feelings. After the meeting the CEO reiterated his decision would stand and sincerely reminded Earp his decisions always would be nonreversible and nonnegotiable.

Earp recognized the will of the CEO would be done and dutifully accepted his position as Special Assistant to the Director of Security.

As he poured himself a cup of coffee, Hoover said, "Are you convinced it's genuine?"

"I reviewed the information, Ed," said Morse. "Marconi and Tesla prepared some very comprehensive findings. I feel beyond any reasonable doubt it warrants your division's intervention."

"Can you brief us on the background?" asked Earp.

Marconi set down the powdered donut he'd been eating and opened the folder in front of him. Reviewing his notes he said, "The incomplete messages have been coming in at the same time for the past several days. I sort of stumbled upon it and would normally have passed it on to an apprentice, but something about it drew me to it. Tesla scanned the passion level and it was off the chart."

Picking up the conversation, Tesla added, "It was quite remarkable, sir. Disjointed and sporadic as it was, every fragment maintained a steady one hundred per-cent."

Hoover's expression told the men they had his attention. "That is unusual," he said. "Generally, the inability to transmit a complete message is due to either infirmity or a complete lack of physical strength."

"That's our feeling, Ed," said Morse. "We know she's an elderly woman who has been seeing her doctor. We also know she's been advised to get her affairs in order."

"By whom?" asked Ness.

"That's why we would like to trace the message," said Morse. "It might probably be her lawyer or even a greedy heir. If that's the case, we could take our time and stay with regular procedure."

Hoover sat back and folded his arms across his chest. "If you two were convinced this was normal financial housekeeping we wouldn't be sitting here," he said.

There was an awkward silence. Tesla and Marconi shifted in their seats.

Morse cleared his throat and said, "That's true," said Morse. "We feel the transmission suggests a catastrophic illness or imminent death."

"Either which are grounds to request a tracer," said Hoover.

Morse, Marconi and Tesla all slightly nodded their heads. Hoover looked at Earp and Ness. "Gentlemen. What's your opinion?" he asked.

"I think it meets the criteria," replied Earp.

"So do I," added Ness.

"Then we seem to be in agreement," said Hoover. "Permission to enact a tracer is granted. I'll have the paperwork processed immediately. When do you want the tracer?"

Marconi and Tesla looked to Morse. Morse cleared his throat and said, "We'd like it in place by early this evening."

Hoover's expression was somber. It was several seconds before he moved. Morse, Marconi and Tesla all felt they overstepped their bounds with such a bold request. Hoover stood up and extended his hand to the men. "Consider it done," he said.

After Marconi and Tesla shook Hoover's hand, Morse grasped it and said, "Thank you, Edgar. We'll report our findings to you ASAP."

Hoover rose from the table and shook each man's hand, a sure sign the meeting was over.

Morse, Marconi and Tesla left Hoover's office and walked down the hallway to the elevators. Marconi pushed the down button and the men waited for the car to reach their floor. When it did, the doors opened and the men were face to face with another high ranking member of security. He was wearing mirrored sunglasses and had a corncob pipe clenched between his teeth. "Good morning General MacArthur," said Morse.

Without answering, MacArthur snapped off a quick salute and briskly walked down the hall. The men stepped into the elevator and Tesla pushed the button for their floor. As the doors closed and the elevator began its descent, he said, "I've been giving the tracer a lot of thought. Why do we need permission to use it? It's not as though we're spying on anybody. They're the ones that come to us. Why do we have to go through the chain of command to retrieve messages that are meant for us?"

"Policy is policy," replied Morse. "Up here in Heaven or down there on Earth, we angels still have to follow the rules."

CHAPTER III

THAT EVENING Tesla and Marconi were relieved of their normal duties and assigned as special liaisons to the tracer division of security. They had joined Morse at a restricted console separate from the other communication receivers. At the moment they were locked in on the frequency that had been providing the previous day's broken messages.

While they were scanning, Morse pulled up a chair and plugged his headphones into the operating system. "Have you heard anything, yet?" he asked.

Marconi shook his head. "Not yet, but this was the time I first received it."

"Mortals are predictable," said Morse. "Their evening prayers always seem to come in at the same time, particularly if the sender is elderly."

"Are you speaking from experience, Sam?" kidded Tesla.

Morse smiled at his friend's remark. "Very funny, hotshot. If I remember correctly you were no spring chicken when you died. You were almost ninety if memory serves."

"I would have made it, too," remarked Tesla. "But I figure working for that slave driver Edison took at least three years off my life."

"Where did he end up?" asked Marconi.

"Where do you think?" replied Marconi. "He transferred over to research and development."

All three enjoyed the levity. Their laughter was interrupted by an incoming message.

"Be quiet you guys," ordered Morse. "She's trying to get through."

"...Father who resides in Heaven."

"It's still broken up," whispered Tesla.

"Not to worry," replied Marconi. "This is what's supposed to happen. Hoover said the tracer will pick up everything we can't hear."

"Are we recording?"

Marconi rechecked the instruments. "Everything's in order," he replied.

The men listened to bits and pieces for several minutes always keeping an eye on the passion meter. For the duration of the message it held steady at one hundred percent.

"... saved me from dying on the RMS Titanic. Amen."

Immediately after hearing amen, the men watched the passion meter fall to zero. "That was quite a prayer," said Morse.

Nodding in agreement Tesla said, "I hope we got it all."

"If Hoover said it would work then it will work," replied Morse. "Rewind the prayer, Guglielmo and let's see what we have."

Marconi reset the prayer and pushed the PLAY setting. The men listened intently as a woman's voice was replayed in their head phones, as clearly as if she were sitting next to them.

"Dear Lord, please hear the prayer of your humble and faithful servant Kathleen O' Hara. Let my cry come to you, dear Father who resides in Heaven. May I remind you I never ask for much, so I am hoping you will answer my prayer. I am an old, old woman who is about to reach her final reward. My body is failing and my doctor said there isn't much more he can do other than to keep me comfortable. In other words, it's time to get my affairs in order. Not my financial ones, but my spiritual ones.

As you know, I survived the sinking of the Titanic. I was only an infant and have no memory of the event. All I know is what I've been told ever since I was old enough to understand. My father, Patrick Dolan got me into a lifeboat that terrible night. My mother passed away during my birth and we were on that cursed ship to begin a new life in America. I've been told by other survivors my father was a hero. Witnesses said my Daddy shook his fist at death and dared him to try and stop him in his attempt to save me.

I know it's in your power Dear Father to answer my prayer. Please help a dying old woman. Please give me the understanding. Please give me the peace. Please give me the vision to see how he kept me from dying on the RMS Titanic. Amen."

The men sat in stunned silence. A tear ran down Marconi's cheek. He was particularly sensitive to any matters dealing with the doomed ship. It was his newly invented wireless telegraph that broadcast the distress messages from the ill-fated liner.

"You don't get too many prayers like that," said Tesla.

"Is that all there is?" asked Marconi.

Morse shook his head. "No, while we were listening the data banks were compiling additional information." He reached over and keyed in the request to access the computer's files. Almost instantly the information the tracer compiled on Kathleen O'Hara was on the viewing monitor.

Name: Kathleen Dolan O'Hara *
Born: August 16, 1911
Place of birth: Dublin, Ireland

Father: Patrick Dolan-deceased

Mother: Theresa Dolan- deceased

Married: June 15, 1929 to William O'Hara-deceased

Children: 6

Grandchildren: 23

Great grandchildren: 40

Current residence: 48 Garfield Place, Brooklyn, New York

"She's ninety seven years old," observed Tesla. "She's got to be one of the last Titanic survivors."

"If not the very last," said Marconi.

Tesla noticed a flashing asterisk next to her name. "Uh oh," he said.

"I see it, too," replied Morse. "She's going to be joining us someday soon."

"Any idea of how long she's got?" asked Marconi.

Morse slowly shook his head. "I haven't got a clue. That's the CEO's decision. Only He knows."

"What are we going to do now?" asked Marconi.

Reaching for a phone Morse said, "Our job is to monitor prayers and forward the legitimate ones to their respective Saints. You guys fax the findings over to Hoover while I give Elmo a call."

"Are we going to have to get in touch with the CEO?" asked Tesla excitedly. He had been in Heaven for over fifty years and still hadn't personally met God.

Morse thought for a moment then replied, "I honestly don't think so. This shouldn't have to get that high up. She isn't asking for a major miracle, only a special gift. I'm pretty sure Saint Elmo's office will be able to handle it."

"Are you sure Elmo is the right Saint for the job?" asked Marconi. "Technically, they were travelers aboard the Titanic. Perhaps Christopher is the one we should be asking."

"If it happened on land I would agree with you," replied Morse. "But since it happened on water I'm sticking with Elmo."

Morse punched in the number to Saint Elmo's office and waited for the secretary to answer. While he waited he printed the bio on Kathleen O'Hara and faxed it to Hoover's office along with a note of thanks for providing the tracer.

Saint Elmo's secretary finally answered the phone. Morse cleared his throat and said, "This is Samuel Morse calling from communications. I'd like to set up an immediate appointment with the Saint."

"I'm sorry Mr. Morse," she replied. "The Saint is booked up until early next week."

Remembering the flashing asterisk after Kathleen O'Hara's name, Morse said, "I may not have until next week. Please fit me in ASAP."

"I understand Mr. Morse, however, I'll be needing confirmation from Mr. Hoover's office."

"You'll have it," promised Morse. "Squeeze me in and it will be on your desk first thing in the morning."

"I can tell by your voice how important this must be to you, Mr. Morse," said the secretary. "I'll see you have a few minutes with Saint Elmo tomorrow morning at eleven."

Morse thanked the secretary and hung up the phone. Turning to Tesla and Marconi he said, "Tomorrow morning at eleven. Can you guys make it?"

"I wouldn't miss it for all the rheostats in the world," exclaimed Tesla.

Marconi was just as thrilled. "Count me in, too," he said.

CHAPTER IV

MORSE, TESLA, AND Marconi were seated in the reception area outside Saint Elmo's office. His secretary was stationed at her desk outside his door. She was a flurry of activity answering phones, setting appointments, typing memos, and faxing messages.

She was on the phone when her intercom buzzed. Putting her party on hold, she transferred to another line and said, "Yes, sir." Looking at the three men she added, "They're right here. Shall I send them in? Yes, sir." Smiling at the three men she said, "Saint Elmo will see you now."

The men rose from their chairs and walked towards Saint Elmo's office. Just as Morse was about to knock on the door, it was opened and the men were greeted by Saint Elmo.

"Gentlemen, it is so nice to see you," said Saint Elmo in a booming voice. "Come in, come in."

Saint Elmo was an enormous barrel-chested man with a thick white beard. His eyes were bright blue and twinkled as though he had just heard a funny joke. He warmly greeted his guests and vigorously shook their hands. Each man discovered that shaking hands with Saint Elmo was like shaking hands with a belt sander. His hands were enormous and heavily callused.

"Please, sit down and make yourself at home, gentlemen," said Elmo.

As the men sat down, Elmo said, "Hoover briefed me on your situation. I must say it's interesting. A very interesting case indeed."

"We feel it satisfies all the specific requirements for an H.I." stated Morse.

"H.I.?" whispered Tesla to Marconi.

"Heavenly Intervention," relied Marconi.

"Am I to assume that you want to handle this yourself?" asked Elmo.

Morse shook his head. "I'm understaffed as it is, sir. I couldn't spare anyone from my department."

Elmo rolled the end of his mustache between his thumb and forefinger. "I see," he said. "Perhaps it would be better to enlist the service of a novice or two. It could prove to be an excellent opportunity."

"A great way to get their feet wet," cracked Tesla who was rewarded with a glare from Morse.

Tesla's humor wasn't wasted on Saint Elmo. He stiffed a laugh by clearing his throat and said, "I'm going to take your word on this, Samuel. At the moment, I'm extremely busy. I've got a Russian sub down in the Barents Sea and I'm being overwhelmed with prayers from the sailor's families. I'll green light this so you can get started right away."

"Thank you, sir," replied Morse.

Saint Elmo punched in his secretary's extension and spoke into the phone.

"Gloria, connect me to personnel, would you please?"

After a moment Elmo said, "This is Elmo over in Dispensation. May I please speak with Saint Joseph?"

While he was waiting to be connected, Elmo said, "As far as I'm concerned, Joseph's got the toughest job in Heaven. The patron Saint of workers covers just about everybody.

"Hello, Joseph? It's Elmo. How are you doing you old slave-driver? That's great. Me? I'm fine. What's that? Yeah, I know. Well, maybe with the United States help they'll be able to get the sub off the bottom and give the bodies a proper burial."

Elmo covered the phone's mouthpiece and said to Morse.

"Peter just called Joseph and said he's processing the souls. They've been arriving steadily for the past few hours. Poor fellows, I hope they didn't suffer too much."

Uncovering the phone, Elmo returned his attention to Joseph. "I need a little help, Joe. I'm granting an H.I. and I was wondering if you could send me over a couple of your sharper apprentices to J. Edgar Hoover's office. You can? Thanks, Joe. He'll be waiting to meet them. If you ever need a favor from me, don't be afraid to ask. Thanks again. Good-bye Joe."

Elmo accessed his secretary's extension and spoke into the phone. "A meeting is being arranged at Hoover's office. Please call him to confirm and that they'll need to be prepped for the meeting."

Elmo hung up the phone then sat at the edge of his desk. "Once the apprentices get here, I want you to bring them, Sam. It'll be up to you to decide if they can handle the assignment. If you think they can, we can send them down to Earth immediately."

Turning to Marconi and Tesla, Elmo said, "Thank you gentlemen. Your work has been invaluable. You can return to your stations and I promise you'll be kept in the loop on this."

CHAPTER V

APPRENTICE ANGELS KYLE Murphy and Ellen Mitchell were in the cafeteria when they heard the public address call their names. It was not uncommon for angels to be air paged, so little notice was given to them by the other diners.

When they heard their names, they took their trays back to the kitchen annex and stepped into the hall.

Murphy was tall and lean and 35 in Earth years. He was handsome and was considered a most eligible bachelor during his later life.

Ellen was older, 64 in Earth years. She was widowed at an early age and went to work as an insurance claims adjuster to support her two children. She worked for 40 years at Gibraltar Insurance and passed away from complications due to a stroke three weeks before her retirement.

They were met by the door by a member of security who handed them each a thick manila envelope. "Would you come with me, please?" he said. "In your hands are your dossiers. You'll need them for your briefing with Director Hoover."

Murphy and Ellen exchanged puzzled looks. They both realized they were in training, but didn't feel their first assignment would be this early.

"Can you tell us what this about?" asked Murphy. Murphy was greeted with a silence that told him he would have to wait for an answer to his question. The angel accompanying them wasn't about to provide any information.

The three walked in silence all the way to the Office of Security. Once there, Murphy and Ellen were turned over to another member of security who ushered them inside.

They were briskly escorted through the reception area and into the office of J. Edgar Hoover.

The moment Murphy and Ellen were inside the office, their escort stepped back out and closed the door behind him leaving the angels with Hoover and Morse.

Hoover was seated behind his desk and Morse was seated on a sofa. Both men stood at the arrival of their guests. Hoover came from behind his desk and offered his hand in greeting. After Hoover introduced himself, it was Morse's turn. Both apprentices were honored and slightly nervous about being summoned by two such important men.

Hoover motioned for the apprentices to sit down. Morse sat back down, but Hoover elected to stay standing, slowly pacing the room as he spoke.

"I'm sure you're both wondering why you've been summoned."

"I tried to get a hint from the man that brought us here, but he wouldn't budge," said Murphy.

"Not if he wants to continue working for me," replied Hoover.

"Please sir," said Ellen. "Is there anything we've done wrong?"

Hoover smiled and said, "On the contrary, Mrs. Mitchell. You're here because you've been doing everything right. Saint Joseph assures me you're both tops in your class and ideal for what I have in mind."

Murphy and Ellen were noticeably relieved. Murphy let out the breath he had been holding and said, "May I ask what that is, sir?"

"Certainly," replied Hoover. "Sam, would you like to take over?"

"Thank you, Edgar," said Morse. "Recently we received a prayer from an elderly lady that was so sincere, we have decided to answer it."

"Wow," whispered Murphy. "And you need our help?" Murphy had recently learned about the process of answering prayers and knew that only the heartfelt ones were answered. Most of the prayers received by

Heaven were for very selfish reasons and were quickly overlooked. A person's prayer to discover pirate's treasure while building a sandcastle with his son would be dismissed, while a person praying for the quick recovery of an ill loved one would in all probability have his prayer answered.

"The request came from Saint Elmo, himself," said Hoover.

Murphy's eyes widened in excitement. To have a Patron Saint involved, the prayer must be extraordinary.

"Elmo is the Patron Saint of sailors," stated Ellen.

"Precisely," said Morse. "Down in New York City, there's a dear old lady, who was on the Titanic when it struck an iceberg. Before the ship could sink, she was put into a lifeboat by her father. Gentleman as he was, he stayed with the ship until she went down. She was only an infant at the time and has no recollection of the tragedy. But, throughout her life she was made aware of his heroics by other survivors. The fellow had quite an adventure and the woman is lucky to be alive. Her prayer is to know what happened. Since we have the capability, we've decided to do it. We're going to answer her prayer."

"But that would require retro-reflection," exclaimed Murphy. "That's Heavenly Intervention."

"You're a fast study," remarked Hoover. "No wonder Joseph recommended you for the job."

"You really want us to take part in an H.I.?" asked Ellen.

"Yes we do," answered Morse. "Can we count on your help?"

Apprentice Angels Murphy and Mitchell answered "Yes" as one.

Hoover returned to his desk and sat down. "Now that that's settled I'll need your dossiers," he said.

Murphy and Ellen placed the envelopes on his desk. They retuned to their seats as Hoover scanned their files.

"Mr. Murphy, it says here you were a fireman."

"Yes, sir."

"And that you were killed in a back draft?"

"That's what I was told, sir. The hall looked stable but somehow my attention was diverted. I never saw it coming."

"You were also cited for bravery several times."

Hoover's praise made Murphy slightly uncomfortable. He was proud of his Earthly citations, but never made a big deal out of them. "I guess it came with the job, sir."

Hoover set down Murphy's file and picked up Ellen's. He read it and said, "Forty years, spotless record!"

"Thank you, sir," replied Ellen.

"As a senior claims adjuster, you had a large amount of discretionary power, didn't you?" asked Hoover.

"Yes, sir."

"And you never abused this power?"

"Sir?"

"You know. Playing with company money. Padding claims. Giving insureds the benefit of the doubt?"

Ellen thought about the question and knew fibbing to Heaven's Director of Security would be useless.

"The insureds always came before company profit, sir. Not many claims people felt that way, but I did."

"Relax, Mrs. Mitchell. It's a quality I find refreshing. You'll be just fine."

"Here's what we're going to do," said Morse. "You two are going down to Brooklyn and interact with Mrs. O'Hara. You are not, repeat not, to keep your identities a secret. You'll have to convince her you're angels which may not be as easy as you think.

"Why not?" asked Murphy.

"We've discovered that while Christians believe in the Father and the Son, there is a certain reluctance to believe in angels. At times I feel like we're the second class citizens of Heaven."

"I could convince her by keeping the Titanic afloat," said Murphy.

"That's where we draw the line," said Hoover. "Your acceptance by her must be spiritual. Is that understood? Any deviation will not be tolerated. I can already

SCOTT MUNSON

tell you, at times you will be very tempted to intercede. But the consequences could be catastrophic. Even the slightest wrinkle in time could cause a shock wave that could change history and that will be avoided at all costs. You're actions will be closely monitored at all times. The only way I can say this is, even though you'll be in a position to save that ship and every life on it, the Titanic will sink. Do you read me? The Titanic will sink and you will do nothing to prevent it."

A tear rolled down Ellen's cheek. "Those poor people," she whispered.

Murphy handed her his handkerchief and said, "When do we leave?"

"Just as soon as we finish your briefing," replied Morse.

Forty five minutes later, Hoover placed a call to Saint Elmo. When the call was completed he hung up the phone and motioned Murphy and Ellen to the center of the room. At that moment, the apprentice angels began to fade. Before Hoover and Morse could wish them luck, they had disappeared and were on their way to Earth.

CHAPTER VI

BENNY EPSTEIN SAT behind the wheel of
his taxicab. He was double parked on Garfield
Place and waiting for a fare he would be taking into
Manhattan.

While looking into his rearview mirror he saw what
he told himself had to be an optical illusion. As if by
magic, where once had been empty space was now occu-
pied by two people who seemed to appear out of thin air.

Benny quickly shook his head to clear the cobwebs
he felt were causing the illusion. He blamed the sudden
appearance of the people on his restless night's sleep and
promised himself a cup of strong black coffee after dropping off the fare.

Ellen and Murphy took a moment to gather in their
surroundings. Garfield Place was a charming street near
Brooklyn's Prospect Park. The residents lived in well
maintained brownstones that were within walking distance of historic Flatbush Avenue.

Murphy checked his notepad for the address of Kathleen O'Hara. It was 48 and saw it was right in front of them.

"How's that for accuracy," he said. Putting the note-book into his breast pocket he took Ellen by the arm to lead her up the steps to the front door.

"Let's not be too hasty," she said. "We have to convince her of whom we are and where we're from. We don't want to scare her with any over-aggressive behavior."

"With what we know about her, she'll have to believe we're angels," said Murphy impatiently. "Either that or we're the greatest mind readers since the Amazing Kreskin."

"In any event, I'd be most appreciative if you'd let me do the talking."

"Right," replied Murphy. "And I'll be the strong, silent type."

"Harpo Marx silent I hope," teased Ellen.

"Gee, Hoover was right," said Murphy.

"Right about what?"

"You are older."

The angels enjoyed the laugh as they climbed the steps from street level. Murphy grabbed the lobby's door handle and pulled. The door remained closed. He tried again and pulled so hard the door rattled in its frame.

"What's the problem with this stupid door," he said.

"This is New York City," replied Ellen. "Anybody who leaves their door unlocked is asking for trouble. We need a key to get into the foyer."

"Allow me," said Murphy. He pointed his index finger at the lock and turned his wrist a quarter turn. As he did, he turned the door handle and pushed open the door.

"Very nice work," commented Ellen.

Stepping aside, Murphy held the door open to allow Ellen entry into the lobby. Bowing slightly at the waist, Murphy said, "T'was nothing, m'lady. After you."

Following Ellen into the lobby, Murphy allowed the door to close behind them.

"She's in apartment 1," said Ellen. "That'll be on the left side of the hallway."

Noticing another door to the hallway, Murphy blew on the tip of his index finger as though he was blowing the smoke away from a recently fired pistol.

"I've got my handy-dandy key all warmed up," he said.

"Not this time, Willie Sutton," replied Ellen. "We'll scare her half to death if we start knocking on her door. She'll know we'd have bypassed security measures to get there."

Murphy didn't care for the prospect of being so easily thwarted. "So what do we do now?" he said. "Wait here until she decides to take her daily jog through the park?"

"I'll show you what we do now," said Ellen patiently. She pushed the intercom button to Kathleen O'Hara's apartment.

After several moments came a response. "Who is it?" asked a female voice from the speaker. The angels realized it was not the voice of an elderly woman.

"We're from Medicare," replied Ellen. "We're conducting a routine audit of bills paid on Kathleen O'Hara's behalf to Dr. Ferguson."

"How did you get into the lobby?" asked the voice.

"The door was open, Ma'am," replied Ellen. "May we please have a moment with Mrs. O'Hara?"

There was a long silence over the intercom. Murphy was about to push the button when a voice came over the speaker. "I'll buzz you through, but I'll want to see some ID outside the door."

"Absolutely," replied Ellen.

A loud buzz filled the lobby. The lock was deactivated and Ellen pulled the door open. Murphy and she stepped through the door way and walked past the stairwell. As they walked down the hall, Murphy whispered, "I'm impressed you got us this far, but they're going to want to see ID. What are you going to do about that?"

The angels were outside the door to apartment 1. Ellen knocked on the door and turned to Murphy. "We're going back to the Titanic and you're worried about a couple pieces of laminated cardboard? Look in your right pocket."

Murphy stuck his hand into his pocket and pulled out a flawless photo ID of himself as an auditor with Medicare. He watched as Ellen pulled a similar ID of her from her purse.

From the other side of the door came the voice. "Please step back from the door and display your IDs at peephole level. The angels stepped to the center of the hall and held up their ID. After a moment, they heard unmistakable sounds of locks being thrown.

The door to Kathleen O'Hara's apartment opened and the angels stood face to face with her day attendant. She was a pleasant looking young woman. With long blond hair tied into a ponytail, Ellen guessed her age to be in the early twenties and was perhaps a college student or a great grand daughter."

"Good morning," said Ellen. "My name is Ellen Mitchell and this is my associate Kyle Murphy. May we come in?"

"Sure," replied the attendant. "Come in, and have a seat at the kitchen table. My name is Julie Barlowe. I work for an agency that provides care and companionship for the elderly. I've worked for Mrs. O'Hara for almost a year now. She's napping at the moment; she'll be disappointed if she sleeps through the Price Is Right."

"You're so young to be a nurse," said Ellen.

"Oh, I'm not a nurse," replied Julie. "I'm more of a companion. I mean I can help her with her medications and things like that. But mostly, I'm here to cook for her, help her in the bathroom, and keep her company. Things are so hard for her in that wheelchair."

Ellen smiled warmly at Julie and said, "You're such a dear for taking such good care of her."

Any reservations Julie had about her visitors melted away when Ellen smiled at her. "Thank you," replied Julie. "She really is a remarkable woman. In case you didn't know, she was on the Titanic. She's probably the last living survivor. She was only a baby. She loves to talk about how her father saved her life."

"I'm sure she would," agreed Murphy.

"Lately, though, she just doesn't seem to be herself," said Julie. "She seems to be failing right before my eyes."

"We all begin to fail as we get older," offered Ellen.

Julie shook her head. "Not physically or even mentally. She's still as sharp as a tack. She's failing emotionally. She seems as though she's lost the will to live. It started about a week ago."

Ellen and Murphy looked at each other, each remembering Heaven began receiving Kathleen O'Hara's prayers at about that time.

"Of course I may be wrong, and I hope I am, but I think she may have gotten some bad news from her doctor."

"She hasn't mentioned anything to you?" said Murphy.

"No, she's so sweet. She says she doesn't want to bore me with all the details about her health problems. I guess she saves all that for the night nurse."

"When does the night nurse arrive?" asked Ellen.

"At 6:00 PM sharp," replied Julie. "By that time, we've had dinner, the kitchen has been straightened up, and Mrs. O'Hara is in her pajamas."

Murphy looked at his watch. It was almost 11:00 AM. If their plan was going to work, they would need Julie out of the picture. Taking the initiative, Murphy stood up and said, "Would you mind if I helped myself to a glass of water?"

"No problem," replied Julie. "The glasses are in the cupboard to the left of the sink."

Murphy went to the sink and filled up a glass with water. Returning to the table, he sat the glass down and stood behind Julie. He gently placed his fingertips to her temples. Julie immediately stopped talking mid-sentence and remained in position as though she was flash frozen.

"Nice work," said Ellen admirably. "We've got to make her think its six o'clock and she's being relieved by the night nurse."

"That shouldn't be too difficult," said Murphy. "I'll step outside while you work in here. You make her think and feel its 6:00PM. Plant the suggestion that until she wakes up tomorrow morning, it is seven hours later than it really is. After you've done that, vanish and wait for me. I'll return as a substitute night nurse and Julie will leave thinking everything is normal. As soon as she leaves, you can reappear."

At that moment, every clock in the apartment shifted to 6:00PM and the sunset faded to an early evening intensity visible only to Julie Barlowe.

Ellen thought the plan over and nodded in approval. "I'm going to wake her up now."

"Ready when you are," said Murphy. "Give me a minute to get out." Murphy exited the apartment and waited outside for his cue.

As Murphy waited in the lobby, Ellen gently blew on Julie's face, and then disappeared. As soon as she did, Julie reanimated with no memory of ever meeting and speaking with the angels. As far as she knew, it was 6:00PM and time for her relief to be arriving.

Noticing the glass on the table she said, "That's funny. I don't remember pouring a glass of water." The water was quickly forgotten as the intercom buzzed. Julie went to the intercom. "Who is it?"

"Visiting nurse service," replied Murphy in a female voice.

Julie deactivated the lock and said, "Come on in."

She waited at the door and peered out of the peephole. She watched as a pretty blond woman with a large, toothy smile entered her field of vision. Opening the door, Julie said, "You're new. What happened to Connie?"

"She called in sick at the last minute," said the nurse.

"I'll be replacing her until she's back on her feet."

Julie invited the nurse into the apartment. After she stepped in, Julie said, "You look familiar to me. Do we know each other?"

"Not that I know of," replied the nurse. "This is my first time in this part of Brooklyn."

"I could swear I've seen you before," said Julie. "I rarely forget a face. Oh well, maybe it'll come to me later. Let me say good-bye to Mrs. O'Hara and I'll be on my way."

Julie went into the living room expecting to find Kathleen dressed for bed and watching the news. Instead, she found her asleep in an easy chair, her wheelchair close beside her. Julie returned from the living room with a puzzled expression on her face.

"That's funny, she's not ready for bed. How did I let the time slip away?" Julie looked at the clock on the kitchen wall and saw it was 6:03PM.

"That's okay," said the nurse. "She must have kept you hopping today. You go home now and get some rest. I'll be glad to get Mrs. O'Hara ready for bed."

"Thank you. I think I will go home now," said Julie absently. She took her coat from the closet, put it on and went to the door. Before leaving she turned and said, "Are you sure we've never met?"

The nurse shook her head and said, "I don't think so because I'm sure I would have remembered you."

"It's just that you look so familiar. Anyways, thanks for taking care of Mrs. O'Hara. You have a nice evening and I'll see you tomorrow morning."

"Thank you. I will."

As soon as Julie left the apartment, the nurse closed the door and returned to the kitchen. When she walked in, she saw Ellen sitting at the table.

"Oh for crying out loud," said Ellen.

Remembering Ellen was seeing him as a female nurse, Murphy quickly morphed back to his angelic self. "Ahh! That's better. That girdle was killing me. What's the matter with you?" he asked.

"Do you think it was the wisest thing in the world to turn yourself into Hot Lips Houlihan? What if Julie was a big fan of M*A*S*H*?"

"I couldn't help it," said Murphy. "Loretta Swit was the only nurse I could think of on such short notice."

"Do me a favor," said Ellen. "When you're back on the Titanic, don't change yourself into Leonardo DiCaprio."

Murphy chuckled and replied, "That wouldn't make a difference. The Titanic sank over sixty years before Leo was born. To anybody on that ship, he'd just be another face in the crowd."

Ellen slowly nodded her head in approval at Murphy's logical observation. "Well put Mr. Murphy. Well put, indeed. For the first time today you have actually…"

"Julie, is that you?" said Kathleen O'Hara from the living room.

Ellen stood up from the table and looked at Murphy. She tried to appear confident but Murphy could tell she was as nervous as he was. "They just rang the bell for round two," she said. "Are you ready?"

"As ready as I'll ever be," said Murphy as they walked toward the living room.

Morse, Marconi, and Tesla leaned closer to the monitor they were watching. The men were in Morse's office watching the proceedings from Earth. Additional optical feeds of the angel's quest were also being viewed by representatives from Hoover's and Saint Elmo's respective offices.

"Here's where it gets interesting," said Hoover.

"I thought Murphy may have spoiled things when the aid almost recognized him," said Tesla.

"I think if Julie had been 10 years older, she might have," added Marconi. "Murphy's lucky M*A*S*H* was before her time."

"Regardless of that minor hitch, they've done a superior job so far."

"What's next on the agenda?" asked Tesla.

"Here's where they meet Mrs. O'Hara. They have to convince her they're there to answer her prayer."

"They're there to answer her prayer? You're a poet, but you don't know it." quipped Marconi.

Morse gave Marconi a glare. "Hush up, will you? They're about to meet Mrs. O'Hara."

CHAPTER VII

THE ANGELS STEPPED into the living room and saw Kathleen O'Hara sitting in her chair. She was a tiny woman, with thin, wispy white hair. Most of her scalp was visible through what was left of her hair.

Her skin was heavily wrinkled and was covered with age spots. Peering through enormously thick glasses were vivid green eyes.

Ellen guessed the woman couldn't weigh much more than eighty pounds. She was dressed in a heavy sweater, sweat pants, and fluffy bedroom slippers. Around her shoulders was draped a knit shawl. A blanket covered her lower body.

Murphy and Ellen smiled warmly at Kathleen. Ellen extended her hand in greeting. She didn't take Kathleen's hand, not wanting to risk hurting her by squeezing too hard. Instead she let Kathleen take hers.

"Where's Julie?" asked Kathleen. "It can't be 6:00 already."

"No, dear. It's not. We sent Julie home for the day. We're going to keep you company today. My name is Ellen and this is my friend Kyle."

Kathleen looked at Murphy warily. He noticed her unease and extended his hand. Kathleen placed her hand on his and the anxiety she felt, disappeared. "Are you from the visiting nurse service?" she asked.

The angels looked at each other for a moment. Murphy shrugged his shoulders and said, "No, Ma'am, we're not."

Kathleen swallowed and tried to talk but the words got stuck in her throat. The angels mistook her excitement for fear. Ellen immediately dropped to her knees so to speak to Kathleen at eye level. "Please don't be afraid, dear. Kyle and I are here to help you in ways you can't imagine."

Tears streamed down Kathleen's face. She took off her glasses and set them in her lap. Taking out a tissue from the cuff of her sweater she wiped her damp cheeks. "But that's not true," whispered Kathleen in a broken voice. "I've imagined help in many ways, praying it will come."

"We know," said Murphy. "That's why we're here."

Kathleen closed her eyes and clasped her hands bringing them to rest on her chest. "Do either of you two believe in God?" she asked.

"With all our hearts," replied Ellen.

"Do you also believe that God answers all prayers?"

"Not all,' said Murphy. "Only the ones worth answering. Your recent prayer was very powerful. It touched us deeply."

Kathleen opened her eyes and looked at the angels. On her face was a look of pure joy. "What's it like? Is it beautiful? According to my doctor, I'll be able to see for myself shortly. I'm filled with cancer."

Let's not concern ourselves with that, dear. We're here to answer your prayer, and answering your prayer is just what we're going to do."

As delighted as Kathleen was to be in the angels' company, she wanted to give them one more test. "If you are who I think you are, then you'll know what that prayer is."

Murphy smiled and said, "I was wondering when that question would arise. Your prayer is to see how your father got you off the Titanic."

The tears flowed again as Kathleen crossed herself then bowed her head in a silent prayer of thanks.

Morse, Marconi, and Tesla took off their headsets and set them on the desk. Morse reached to the console and turned the volume way down. The prayer was so heartfelt and personal he felt like he was eavesdropping by listening to it. When it was finished he turned the volume back up and the three men put their headsets back on.

"How long have we been doing this?" Tesla said to no one in particular.

"Over fifty years," Marconi replied.

"In all those years, I don't think I've seen anything more touching," Tesla said softly.

CHAPTER VIII

KATHLEEN PUT HER glasses back on and looked at the angels in awed wonder.

"Are we really going back to the Titanic?" she asked.

"In a way," Ellen replied. "Here's what Kyle and I have worked out. He's going to the Titanic, you and I are staying here. The best way for me to explain this is to use television as an example. Kyle will go back to the ship and act as a camera, transmitting a picture signal back to us. I'll be the receiver and screen the image for you."

Kathleen looked at her table-top television and frowned. "It's going to be on T.V.?"

"Much better than television," Murphy said. "Virtual reality."

Kathleen was confused and looked questioningly to Ellen. "Virtual what?"

Realizing such technology was beyond Kathleen's scope of the world, Ellen replied, "It's an amazing sight and sound perception, dear. By what you see and hear, you'll think we're abroad the ship, but we won't be. We'll be right here in the safety of your apartment. You'll see images so lifelike you'll want to reach out and touch them, but they won't be there. All you'll be touching is the air."

Ellen's explanation didn't do much to soothe Kathleen's anxiety. The old woman nervously wrung her hands and said, "Will you be with me? Will you promise you'll stay with me?"

Ellen gently grasped Kathleen's hand and said, "Every moment, my dear. I'll never leave your side. In fact, I'll be the one thing you see that's real. If you need me to, I'll hold your hand every step of the way."

Kathleen took a deep breath, and then slowly let it out. "I'm ready," she said. "Take me back to the Titanic."

The finality of Kathleen's statement caught the angels by surprise. All along their plan had been theory, now it was about to be applied. Knowing his time had come, Murphy went to the center of the room and said, "Well, it looks like this is it. It's now or never. Look for me on the Titanic, ladies."

Before Kathleen's eyes, Kyle began to slowly fade. She removed her glasses and quickly wiped them with a tissue then replaced them, not sure if she could believe her eyes. Before Murphy totally faded away, Kathleen said excitedly, "Kyle? Kyle, please don't go, yet. There's something I need to ask you."

Murphy heard her calling him and materialized before her. "Yes, dear. What is it?"

Kathleen looked at Murphy with wide pleading eyes. "Is what I prayed for really about to happen?"

Murphy was sure he knew what was coming next. With a blank expression he solemnly nodded.

"If that's true, then you could save him. You could save them all."

Murphy slightly shrugged his shoulders and nodded in agreement.

"Would you please save them? It's in your power. Please save them from their terrible fate. God would understand."

Murphy slowly shook his head and said, "God's will is unquestionable and non-negotiable. I'm truly sorry, but there is nothing I can or will do to save the ship." Murphy quickly checked the time and added, "Right now, the R.M.S. Titanic is on a collision course with an iceberg. In a few minutes Frederick Fleet will see that iceberg, but it will be too late. Two hours and forty minutes after that the Titanic will have sunk."

Murphy's words had a chilling effect on Kathleen. For several moments the room remained silent. Ellen thought the journey might have ended before it ever began.

Kathleen cleared her throat and sat upright in her chair. "I understand your position, Kyle. I won't hold it against you or God. I'm sorry for being so selfish and trying to alter so great a gift. Please continue, there'll be no more interruptions from me."

Murphy smiled warmly at Kathleen, and then blew her a kiss as he disappeared. Where he once stood was now empty space.

"He's gone," Kathleen said softly. "He vanished right before my eyes. Is he really on the Titanic?"

Ellen didn't answer her, she was too busy looking around the room and sniffing the air. Coming from every direction in the living room was the unmistakable smell of saltwater, a vast amount of saltwater.

As Murphy faded from their monitor, Marconi turned to Morse and said, "The kid did well. I like the way he held his composure when she asked about saving the ship."

Morse nodded in agreement. "So far, so good. Let's keep an eye on him, though. This next step is crucial."

CHAPTER IX

KATHLEEN SQUEEZED ELLEN'S hand as the apartment was plunged into darkness. Small, bright dots of light began appearing on the ceiling. A few at first, then more and more, each appearing faster than Ellen could count.

To Kathleen it was as though she was sitting under the rotunda of a planetarium as a sky show was beginning. A soft light bathed the apartment in an eerie glow. It was just bright enough to show that where once stood walls, windows, carpeting, and furniture, now stood wooden decking and iron railings. At the far reaches of their vision, they saw the unmistakable image of Kyle looking at his new surroundings in awed wonder. To Ellen, Kyle reminded her of a little boy who was seeing Disneyworld's Magic Kingdom for the first time.

"Saints be praised," Kathleen whispered. "Am I seeing what I think I'm seeing?"

"You are," Ellen replied softly. "That's Kyle and he's on the Titanic."

Marconi let out a sigh of relief. He patted Tesla on the shoulder and said, "He made it. The son of a gun actually made it. What time do we have?"

Tesla checked the lower right corner of the monitor and checked the digital readout set to Titanic time. "Eleven thirty-seven," he replied somberly.

Both men were silent, each knowing that in three minutes they would witness a collision that would start one of the most infamous tragedies in world history.

Murphy couldn't believe his eyes. He was actually on the foredeck of the great ship. From historical accounts, he knew the temperature was bitterly cold, but he felt no discomfort. He slowly let out his breath hoping to see telltale frozen vapors, but there were none.

A quick check of his watch indicated that if he was indeed on the Titanic, the terrific collision would occur in less than three minutes. He sprinted to the bow and grasped the iron railings in the liner's bowsprit pulpit. He looked down at the unbelievably calm ocean and saw and heard the bow slicing through the frigid water. He raised his head and concentrated on the area of ocean directly ahead of the ship. His Divinely assisted vision could see the enormous iceberg floating in the darkness.

There's still plenty of time, he thought. If I could warn them, they could pass it with ease.

Murphy turned and looked at the lookouts in the crow's nest. From their seats in Kathleen's living room, Kathleen and Ellen had the same view. From his viewpoint he could see seamen Fleet and Lee were looking in the proper direction, but without their misplaced binoculars, they wouldn't see the iceberg until it was too late.

"Blimey, 'tis colder 'an a witch's tit," said Lee.

"You can say that again, mate," agreed Fleet. " 'Tis a cold night, indeed,"

" 'Ave you ever seen the sea so calm? An' the stars, surely there must be millions of 'em shining tonight."

Fleet wasn't listening to his friend. It seemed as though he was hearing a faraway whisper. He quickly shook his head and tried to clear his mind. "Whadja say, mate?"

"The stars," Lee replied. "I was sayin' how there must be…"

"No, no, no, before that. Somethin' 'bout icebergs?"

Murphy jumped as the quiet was shattered by a clap of thunder. It boomed from directly over his head. After recovering from the shock he noticed something was dreadfully wrong. His world was frozen in time. He was surrounded by silence and stillness. There was not a sound to be heard. No displaced ocean creating an enormous ship's wake. No drone of the powerful steam turbines. Even the belching smoke from the enormous stacks was stark still.

As an angel Murphy had seen many miraculous things but he wasn't prepared for what was happening. He was witness to absolute suspended animation. Time was literally standing still. To Murphy it was like being stuck in an illustration.

Murphy turned in terror to the sound of a voice booming from the darkness. "One more mistake like that, young fellow and I'll shut this operation down so fast you'll never know what hit you."

Murphy watched as a figure stepped from the shadow. As the figure came into view, Murphy recognized him as Allan Pinkerton, one of J. Edgar Hoover's right hand men in security. Murphy knew Pinkerton was internationally known as the founder of the Pinkerton National Detective Agency and the U.S. Secret Service.

"I'm sorry, sir," Murphy stammered. "What did I do?"

"Don't even think about trying to save this ship, son. Your desire to help these people is admirable, but very dangerous. You unintentionally planted a subliminal warning into lookout Fleet. I'll take care of it, but I don't want anymore mistakes. Fleet will see the iceberg, but not with any help from you. If you can't follow the rules of the assignment, I'll get someone down here who can. Have I made myself clear?"

"Yes, sir," Murphy replied. "Crystal clear, sir."

Murphy thought he detected a slight smile from under Pinkerton's mustache. In a warmer and softer voice, Pinkerton said, "That's just what I wanted to hear. Good luck, son."

Before Murphy had a chance to say another word, Pinkerton disappeared into the air.

"What happened?" Kathleen said. "What was that all about?"

"Security had to interrupt the miracle," Ellen replied. "Kyle almost changed history which we know is forbidden. The same thing would have probably happened to me. Imagine being in the position to actually save the Titanic."

"But I was watching. He didn't say a word to the boys in the crow's nest."

"It was a great inner desire to help," Ellen replied. "It was so strong it carried telepathically. Whatever was accidentally planted in their minds will be erased by Pinkerton. Keep watching."

"Blimey, 'tis colder 'en a witch's tit," said Lee.

"You can say that again, mate," agreed Fleet. " 'Tis a cold night, indeed,"

" 'Ave you ever seen the sea so calm? An' the stars, surely there must be millions of 'em shining tonight."

Fleet didn't respond to Lee's observation. He was staring at the horizon. Something strange was happening. The stars Lee had mentioned were blinking out at the waterline. As his eyes adjusted, he could see they were being hidden by a colossal wall of ice.

"Oh my dear Jesus," whispered Fleet. He grabbed the bell cord and yanked it viciously three times as a warning to the bridge.

Murphy heard the bell ring and began walking toward the stern, away from the bow on the port side. He didn't want to watch as he knew the Titanic would strike the iceberg on the starboard side.

He stopped by one of the ship running lights and checked his watch. It was eleven-forty, PM.

He grabbed the railing and braced for the collision that would claim over 1500 lives and break millions of hearts.

CHAPTER X

PATRICK DOLAN WAS sitting on the edge of his bunk bed, cradling his infant daughter as she drank from her baby bottle in their cramped steerage quarters. The only light in the room came from the hallway via the crack under the door. It was just enough light to let him maneuver the room, not that he needed much light. The only furnishings in the tiny area were a pair of bunk beds, a chest of drawers and a small sink. A blind man could have found his way around the room with no trouble.

Dolan was twenty four years old and carried 220 pounds on a large, muscular frame. He was traveling to America with his infant daughter Kathleen. Dolan's young wife, Margaret, had died during Kathleen's birth. In an attempt to ease his heartbreak, relatives in New York City convinced him to leave Ireland and relocate to Manhattan's lower west side to the tenements of Greenwich Village, with the promise of a job and inexpensive accommodations.   Although reluctant to leave his beloved Ireland, he knew his daughter's best interest was in America.

Lacking any such funds to hire a traveling nurse-maid for Kathleen, Dolan was caring for his daughter himself.   Several other mothers in adjacent rooms noticed Dolan's dilemma and offered to help with her daily care.   Soiled diapers were rinsed in the lavatory commode then laundered in the utility sink.   Although little Kathleen was still on the bottle, she did enjoy a little solid food consisting of soupy mashed potatoes and pulverized vegetables provided at the dining room table. Kathleen's only bottle was an odd looking glass contraption with rubber nipples at both ends.   It was designed for multiple feedings at the same time, but it was the only bottle Dolan had. For Kathleen's bottle feedings, he would keep a small supply of milk in cold tap water in his sink. When Kathleen would awaken in the night, he would fill the bottle with milk then set the remaining milk aside while he emptied the sink.   He would then hold the bottle under hot water until the milk warmed up. When the milk was the proper temperature, he refilled the sink with cold water and set tomorrow mornings remaining milk back into the sink.

Little Kathleen was just about finished with the bottle. Her tiny lips were letting go of the rubber nipple and her breathing was slow and deep, a sure sign to Dolan she was falling back asleep. He glanced at the empty bunk across from him and wondered if he could place Kathleen there. Since their voyage began, Dolan had slept on his side with his back against the wall leaving the rest of the bunk for Kathleen.

The baby pulled her mouth away from the nipple. Satisfied, the infant was fast asleep, he was about to place her in the empty bunk when he felt a vibration through the cabin floor.

"Oh my Lord," whispered Kathleen. "Is that my father? Am I really seeing my father?"

Ellen patted Kathleen's hands and said, "Yes, dear. That's him. That fine young man we're watching is your father. And the baby he's so lovingly caring for is you."

"But it' so dark," commented Kathleen. "I want to see him in the light."

Ellen heard an ominous rumbling. It had started small, but was rapidly building. A feeling of dread fell over her. "I think he'll be turning on a light very shortly," she said.

The vibrations in the cabin increased to an alarming degree. Dolan hoped it was related to the workings of the ships massive engines, but this was entirely different from their steady throb.

He carefully set Kathleen in the bunk then stood up and found he had to balance himself by grabbing onto the upper berth. The vibrations were now so intense that his toilet articles he kept on top of the dresser were sliding towards the edge.

Dolan opened the cabin door and stepped out into the hallway. Nothing seemed out of the ordinary. The only other person in the hall was another passenger he assumed was investigating the disturbance.

The breath hitched in Kathleen's throat. "Lord have mercy!" she gasped. "That's Kyle. How did he get down there? And look at him! His clothes are all different. He's dressed like a peasant. How on Earth did he manage that?"

Ellen didn't want Kathleen's excitement to get the best of her, so she spoke in a gentle, assuring tone. "You're going to see many remarkable things, dear. Yes, that is Kyle. As we explained earlier, he's a transmitter for us. He has to be nearby for your prayer to work. He will want to blend in and he can't very well do that dressed in our times' modern clothing."

As the women watched, Dolan approached Murphy to speak to him about the disturbance. As he neared, Kathleen tensed and squeezed Ellen's hand so hard the angel was surprised by the old woman's sudden strength. "Oh, look at my Daddy, look at my Daddy. He's so handsome. It's the only time I've ever seen him. I never even had a picture to remember him by. Not even a tin type."

"Say, mate," Dolan said. "Didja feel the tremblin' too?"

Murphy nodded and replied, "I sure did. That wasn't any engine malfunction, either. If you ask me, we've struck something."

"Wha' could we ha' struck in the middle of the North Atlantic?" Dolan asked.

Murphy knew the answer, but wisely chose not to reveal it. Dolan must not be given any advantages over the other passengers. Knowing the baby would be saved without Divine intervention made his decision to keep quiet bearable under the mounting trauma.

"I'll go find a steward," Murphy suggested. "I'll ask him what he knows."

"Good idea, mate," Dolan replied. "Wouldja mind doin' me a small favor? Knock on me door an' let me know whatcha find out?"

Murphy quickly shook Dolan's hand and said, "I'll be glad to. I'll be right back."

Dolan watched Murphy trot down the hall then disappear around the corner. He stepped back into his room and noticed the shuddering had stopped. Dolan felt better until he realized it was too quiet. The engines had stopped, their familiar steady hum was no longer heard. Dolan carefully climbed over his sleeping daughter and lay down on his bunk wondering what would have caused the mammoth liner to shut down.

As he lay in the bunk listening for the engines to restart, his tiredness overtook him and he fell back to sleep. It would be the next to last peaceful moment Patrick Dolan would ever enjoy.

CHAPTER XI

DOLAN WAS JOLTED awake by the pounding on his door. Before he could answer it, a steward burst in and turned on the lights. "Life jackets on," he said. "Everyone put your life jackets on and wait in the hall."

Before Dolan could ask what the trouble was the steward was gone, on his way to the next cabin.

The cabin's life jackets were stored on a shelf in a small closet. As Dolan pulled the four life jackets off the shelf he noticed they were all adult sized. Not one of them would fit a small child, let alone an infant. He had a mental note to mention that to someone in authority once they reached New York.

Dolan put the life jackets on the opposite bunk and stepped out into the hall. Throughout the hallway were several small groups of steerage passengers milling about, all wondering why the White Star Line would conduct a drill at such a late hour. It was obvious to

Dolan that they had all been in a deep sleep and had not felt the ship shudder to a stop.

He was about to gather his daughter and seek out a steward when he saw Murphy walking briskly toward him.

"Here comes Kyle," said Ellen. "Uh-oh, this could be a problem."

"What kind of problem?" Kathleen asked.

"Look at his expression," Ellen replied. "Anybody can see he knows something dreadful has happened."

As he approached Dolan, Murphy made a conscious effort to clear his mind of all the catastrophic news he possessed. He changed his fearful expression to one of uncertainty. "I asked a steward what happened," he said.

"What did the steward say?" Dolan asked.

"He said he thinks we threw a propeller blade." Murphy knew this wasn't true, but didn't blame the steward. For all the steward knew, the Titanic was unsinkable.

"It just doesn't make sense," Dolan said. "Those people here think it's a drill. Why would we be puttin' on our life jackets 'cause of a busted propeller?"

Murphy knew what was in store for Dolan and baby Kathleen, but was forbidden to help them in any way. At the moment, gates were being locked to keep the steerage passengers away from the lifeboat decks. Once the first class passengers were evacuated the others could have their chance, or so the ships officers thought.

Most of the passengers in the hall had changed out of their night clothes. The hallway had grown surprisingly quiet as they waited for the further instructions that would never come.

His inability to warn the doomed passengers was weighing heavily on Murphy. He leaned against the wall and impatiently waited with the others. Murphy absently drummed his fingertips on the wall. Before he was aware of what he was doing, he began unconsciously began tapping the tip of his index fingers. Three quick taps, followed by three slow taps, and finally another three quick taps. He repeated the tapping over and over, oblivious to what he was doing.

Marconi smiled at Morse as they watched the scene unfold on their monitor. "That sly son of a bitch," Morse marveled. "Either he's incredibly bright or as dumb as dirt. Does he think we wouldn't know he's tapping out an S.O.S?"

"I don't think he's doing it on purpose," Marconi said. "It's just his subconscious trying to help in any way it can. Besides, in 1912, Save Our Ship was as about as widely used as Latin is today. Even if there was somebody there who knew your code, S.O.S. would be meaningless. The mayday call at the time was C.Q.D., come quickly, danger."

Morse nodded in agreement with Marconi's observation and returned his attention to the monitor.

Dolan grew impatient with all the waiting and pulled out his pocket watch to check the time. As he did, several coins were pulled out of his pocket and landed on the hard hallway floor. Most immediately fell on their sides and lay still, but one landed on its edge and began rolling down the hall. It picked up speed as it headed in the direction of the bow.

The others paid no attention to it, but it concerned Dolan deeply. He dropped on one knee, picked up one of the fallen coins, set it on edge and pushed it away. As did the other, it rolled all the way to the end of the hall.

Dolan stood up and looked gravely at Murphy. The ship must be somehow settling at the bow. The settling was slow because until he dropped the coins the passengers felt no change in the ship's level.

Turning to Murphy, Dolan said, "Didja see that, mate?"

Murphy solemnly nodded.

"Ya know what I think?"

Murphy nodded again.

"Ladies and gentlemen," said Dolan. All the passengers in the hall turned and looked toward Dolan. "I'm hopin' you'll all getcher coats on, bring your life jackets, and join me up top."

Most of the groups didn't want to take their families on what they felt was a wild goose chase and voiced their disapproval at Dolan's suggestion.

"An' tell us boy, why should we do that?" asked an irritated passenger. "Do you know somethin' the bloody crew don't?"

Dolan looked to Murphy for some support. "Aren't you going to help me, mate?"

"You're doing fine, yourself," Murphy replied.

"In case you haven't noticed, we're leaning toward the bow," Dolan said. "I got me a gut feelin' that there's more to this drill than meets the eye."

"If ya don't mind, I'll be taking my orders from the crew," replied another man.

Dolan shook his head in mild disgust. He went into his cabin and before wrapping her up in several blankets he filled Kathleen's bottle with the last of the milk and slipped the bottle into his pocket. Confident she would be comfortable against a change in temperature, he brought her into the hall.

"Those silly fools," said Kathleen. "They're signing their death warrants."

"You mustn't be hard on them," Ellen replied. "They had no idea what was going on. At the time, they still felt perfectly safe. They didn't find out about the danger until it was too late."

"Oh, look," Kathleen said. "There's daddy and…is that me?"

"Yes it is," said Ellen. "You are about to begin your miraculous journey."

Dolan closed the door to his cabin and turned to Murphy. "Are ya goin' to join me, mate?"

"I'm right behind you. Let's go."

"Be sure to tell us in the mornin' 'ow the upper crust lives, matey," said someone jokingly.

Dolan ignored the remark and walked down the hall towards the stairs to the upper decks. Following closely behind was Murphy.

The hallways in steerage were a system of turns that left many of the passengers feeling like they were in a maze. Dolan could navigate the halls by reading the signs and following the arrows. At one point when they reached a cross hall, Dolan took a left while Murphy deliberately made a wrong turn to the right, unseen by Dolan. He briskly ran down the hallway and ducked out of sight.

The hallways were now filling up with more and more steerage passengers. Some, like Dolan, were trying to get to the upper decks to investigate. As the crowd grew larger, Dolan turned to be sure Murphy was still with him. He looked into the crowd and couldn't find him.

CHAPTER XII

"**WHAT DID KYLE** do that for," asked Kathleen incredulously. "He left us to fend for ourselves."

"You're forgetting that he was never there in the first place." Ellen replied. "I'm sure he has a very good reason for separating from them."

Dolan decided not to waste any time trying to relocate Murphy. He was confident they would meet up on the deck. As he walked down a hall he heard a commotion from around the next right hand turn.

As he made the turn, he saw a group of passengers gathered at the bottom of a stairwell. Dolan went to the back of the crowd and looked up the stairwell. Behind a closed collapsible gate were two stewards trying to keep order. The steerage passengers wanted the gates opened, but the stewards steadfastly refused.

One of the stewards looked at Dolan and as their eyes made contact, a shiver of surprise ran down Dolan's back. The steward reminded him of the passenger he was talking with a few minutes ago.

"Ooh," gasped Kathleen. "Did you see that? That steward looked just like Kyle!"

"It was Kyle," replied Ellen. "I think I know what he's up to. We'll probably see him assume several identities before the ship…"

Ellen stopped in mid-sentence, knowing she had already said too much.

Kathleen understood and gently patted Ellen's hand. "Don't worry, dear. Please don't feel you've offended me. After all, I know what's going to happen to the Titanic."

""Whatayer waitin' for, ya limey son of a bitch? A direct order from King Edward? Why dontcha open the frickin' gate?" yelled one of the passengers. His questions were met with immediate approval from the others.

"As I said before," replied the steward. "Go back to the main stairwell and wait for further instructions. You'll find no passage through here."

Dolan noticed only one of the stewards was doing all the talking. The other who looked familiar was standing aside remaining curiously uninvolved. It was this man Dolan wanted to talk to.

"You there," yelled Dolan. "The steward in the back! Are you going to stand there and do nothing? There are woman and children down here who would like to get up top. Are you going to let us through, or keep us down here like caged up animals?"

In a clipped British accent, Murphy replied, "Are you all deaf? Don't you hear what me mate's saying? You'll not get through here."

As the steward spoke Dolan thought he detected a signal from him. The steward had almost imperceptivity cocked his head to the right, Dolan's left.

Dolan looked left and saw it was the direction to the stern. Remembering the coins that rolled to the bow, Dolan was sure the steward was tipping him off with a direction to follow. He looked at the group and realized if it was a signal, he was the only one to receive it. He wanted conformation from the steward, but when he looked up the stairwell for him, he was gone.

Kathleen was puzzled by what she just witnessed. "If he can't help them, why does he even bother to make himself known? All that's going to do is torture my father."

Ellen understood Kathleen's confusion. "I know it seems unnecessary, but Kyle has to be nearby. If he isn't you won't be able to see what's happening. Remember, he's our camera."

If the ship was sinking by the bow, then the stern was where Dolan wanted Kathleen to be. He gave a piercing whistle that caught the crowd's attention. "Listen up, mates," he yelled. "We're gettin' nowhere fast hangin' around here. I'm for movin' on. Are you with me?"

"Not bloody likely, mate," yelled out one of the passengers. "When this gate opens, this is where we'll want to be. This limey arse-hole ain't goin' to keep us down here much longer. Ain't that right, mate?"

The steward didn't reply.

Dolan didn't need to be told twice. He adjusted the blankets around Kathleen and took off toward the stern.

CHAPTER XIII

AS DOLAN MADE his way down the hall, little Kathleen began to stir. He knew it would only be a few moments before she awoke, crying and hungry. He wanted to make it up one more deck before he had to stop and feed her.

Dolan quickened his pace in his journey to the stern. As he briskly walked, he had the unmistakable feeling of going uphill. No longer was it a slight sensation. It was obvious the ship was settling at the bow.

The bloody ship is sinking, he thought. Propeller my arse! That vibration was a collision. How long has it been? Fifteen minutes? Twenty?

Dolan followed the signs directing his way to the staircase to D Deck. As he rounded a corner, he heard several voices yelling for a steward. He also heard the distinct sound of a metal folding gate being violently shaken. He followed the commotion until he came upon several people at a gated stairwell to an upper deck. Two of the men were shaking the gate so violently, Dolan was surprised to see it remaining on its hinges. While they tried to break open the gate, the remaining people shouted for a steward that wasn't coming.

The noise immediately woke up Kathleen and she began to scream out of hunger and fear. One of the women heard the baby crying and offered to hold her in an attempt to calm her down. Dolan accepted her offer and reached into his pocket for the milk.

He gave it to the woman and watched as she placed the nipple into Kathleen's mouth. Relief washed over Dolan as he saw Kathleen immediately stop crying and fall back to sleep as her lips worked the nipple in a rhythmic sucking motion.

The men who had been shaking the gate, tired and stopped to rest. As they turned to face the others, one of them spotted Dolan and said, "Have ya been to mid-ship, mate?"

Dolan nodded his head. "Aye, I was just there. They ain't lettin' nobody up. All the bloody gates are locked. The damned stewards looked the other way when we asked them to open up and let us through."

"At least you had a steward," replied the man. "We can't get none of the bastards to even show up here. We can hear them talkin' as they pass by the stairwell. We know they can hear us, but they just ignore us, the bleedin' limey bastards."

"Maybe if all three of us tried the gate." Dolan suggested.

The man shook his head. "Not likely, mate. She may look flimsy, but she's quite sturdy. We ain't been able to put so much as a bend in her."

Dolan looked at the brass housing that held the gate's locking mechanism. It was shiny and new and did indeed look very strong. He asked the woman feeding Kathleen if she could tend the baby for just a moment as he made a quick search of their surroundings. The woman helping Dolan agreed to tend to Kathleen. He thanked her and told the crowd he would be right back.

He ran down the hall, turned a corner and was out of sight. More than one in the group thought to themselves that Dolan had abandoned his daughter and fled in attempt to save himself.

"Where's he going?" said Kathleen. "He didn't leave me, did he? He couldn't possibly have left me."

The misunderstanding concerned Ellen. The last thing she wanted was for Kathleen to become emotionally upset. She needed her to be in a proper frame of mind to appreciate the miracle they were witnessing. She gently stoked Kathleen's hand.

"There, there, dear. Don't even think that. Your father didn't leave you. The fact you're sitting here proves that."

"Maybe that nice lady saved me."

"We know that's not true," replied Ellen. "There are far too many accounts of your father saving you. He'll be back. Just watch with me."

They watched as Dolan ran down the hall until he found what he was looking for. He stopped at a recession in the wall covered with a glass paned door. Posted over the door was a small sign saying, In Case of Fire. Dolan tried the door and discovered it was locked. Knowing his elbow would be protected by the fabric on his coat, he smashed it through the glass door. After removing the broken glass, he pulled the axe through the door and sprinted back to the gate.

The crowd at the gate saw Dolan approach with the axe and knew what would happen next.

"Stand aside," instructed Dolan. "I want plenty of room to work." The people cleared a path for him and Dolan stepped up to the gate. He drew it back and swung with all his strength. The axe head hissed through the air and struck the gate lock with a metallic clang. Several sparks fell to the floor as metal hit metal. The axe didn't break the housing as much as it disintegrated it. Pieces of metal went air-born as the lock shattered. The crowd howled in delight as Dolan pushed the gate open.

With the stairwell now open, the people began climbing the stairs to D Deck. The woman holding

Kathleen gently returned her to Dolan. As she did, she kissed the baby's forehead and Dolan's cheek.

"Thank you," she said. "Good luck to you both and may God bless you."

Dolan waited until the hallway was clear before he followed the others up the stairwell.

Ellen noticed Kathleen was beaming. Tears were running down the old woman's cheeks as she softly said, "I'm sorry, Daddy. How could I ever have doubted you? I'm sorry to have thought you wouldn't come back for me."

Ellen looked at the now empty stairwell. Dolan and Kathleen were now on D Deck. She looked at Kathleen and thought; You might want to save some of those tears for later, dear. You're going to need them.

Marconi pushed his chair back from his console, stood up and said, "What do you say, Sam? You want to break for lunch?"

Keeping his eye on his console, Morse shook his head and replied, "Not me. I wouldn't miss this for the world. Did you see his resourcefulness? Using that axe to break through the gate? He just saved all those people's lives!"

"Not exactly," said Marconi somberly. "Only the women's. The men all die, remember?"

"Well, at least he gave them hope!"

Marconi decided to stay with Morse and watch the continuing drama. He sat back down and said, "That he did. A fellow can go a long way on hope."

As Dolan and the group he rescued ran down the hallway, they passed the third class dining room. To call it a dining room was being kind, it was more of a feeding area with none of the amenities the upper class passengers enjoyed.

Dolan remembered that Kathleen had finished the little bit of milk he had carried with him. Realizing he would need more, he yelled to the group he was going to stop for a moment to search the galley. The group understood his predicament and offered to help him, but he sent them on their way to the upper deck with the promise to catch up to them.

He stepped into the room and noticed a severe slant in the furnishings. It was no optical illusion. The ship was sinking. Dolan knew it was no longer a matter of "if", but rather, "when".

At the far end of the room he saw two large swinging doors that he knew, having already eaten in the dining hall, led to the galley. He tightened the blankets around his sleeping daughter and moved toward the double doors.

As he did, they swung into the dining hall and Murphy stepped in, dressed as a waiter. Murphy's eyes met Dolan's and Dolan stopped dead in his tracks. He shook his head to clear his vision because he felt he was seeing things. The waiter looked exactly like the steward who had refused him entry to D Deck.

"There's Kyle," exclaimed Kathleen. "Now he dressed up like a waiter."

"He's so clever," marveled Ellen. "First a steward and now a waiter. What will he think of next?"

"Look at my father," said Kathleen. "He looks like he's seen a ghost!"

"Not a ghost, just an angel," replied Ellen. "But his expression does suggest he thinks something strange is going on."

"Will it affect my miracle?" Kathleen asked in alarm.

"I honestly don't know," said Ellen. "I would hope not. We were told we couldn't directly interfere with the course of history, and so far we haven't. Let's keep watching and see what happens next."

Dolan glared at the waiter. "Didn't I see you back at the gate a while ago, mate?"

"No, sir," replied Murphy. "I've been here all night and haven't left my post since we hit the…"

Dolan didn't like the way Murphy cut his sentence short. It scared him, but at the same time steeled him.

"You were about to say something," said Dolan.

"No, sir."

"Bloody hell, you weren't," said Dolan. "What kind a fool do ya' take me for? Anyone can see the ship's sinking! Now what in God's name did we hit? Another ship?

Murphy slowly shook his head and looked at the floor. "We struck an iceberg, sir."

"Have other ships been alerted?" asked Dolan. "Are they on their way?"

"They are, sir. But if I were you, I'd get to the lifeboats just the same."

"But if the ships are on their way, wouldn't it be safer to stay on board. Surely we'll stay afloat until they can…"

A cold certainty covered Dolan like a blanket. "How do ya' know, mate?"

Murphy continued to look at the floor. "I can't tell you, friend. Just keep working your way to the lifeboats."

"I will," promised Dolan. "I just need to stop and get some milk for my daughter."

"There's milk in the iceboxes in the galley," said Murphy. "I'll give you a hand."

Inside the galley, Murphy held Kathleen while Dolan filled her bottle with milk. He slipped the bottle back into his pocket and took Kathleen from Murphy. "She'll be fine for a while, but she'll wake up hungry. I'm glad I'll have this to give to her."

Murphy smiled and led Dolan out of the galley. Pointing toward the hallway, he said to Dolan, "Good luck, sir. May God be with you and your daughter."

"Aren't you coming with me?" asked Dolan.

"Not just now, sir. I'll meet you on deck, later." Murphy turned and walked back into the galley.

Now having the milk his daughter would later need, Dolan left the dining room and continued his journey.

Morse smiled and clapped Marconi on the shoulder. "May God be with you and your daughter. Truer words were never spoken."

"You said it," agreed Marconi. "The Big Guy has been with them the whole time."

CHAPTER XIV

DOLAN THOUGHT HIS best chance at reaching the upper deck would be to return to the main stairwell. Since he had broken through the gate at the lower steerage levels, he assumed since the next deck was C Deck and first class, he would have a clear passage.

He was wrong. He came around a corner and looked down the center hall. Gathered at the bottom of a stairwell was a group of people. A few were members of his original party, but they had been joined by the other immigrants trying to reach the life boats.

As he ran down the hall, one of the women recognized him. "This gate is locked, too!" she yelled. Pointing up the stairwell, she added, "The men are trying to break it down."

Dolan met the group and surveyed the situation. At the top of the stairs, three men were laying their shoulders into the gate, trying to snap the lock. "They need an axe!" yelled Dolan. "We've got to get them an axe!"

"We thought of that," replied the woman. "We searched high and low. All the axes have been taken from their cases. Others must have had the same idea."

Dolan's mind raced. "There's got to be something we can do to…"

He was interrupted by the terrified scream of a woman.

Dolan saw her pointing down the opposite hall. Coming towards them at the speed of a brisk walk was a stream of water. It was several inches deep and could be seen running under cabin doors as it approached the stairwell.

Dolan had an idea. "You say you've searched this area?"

"Aye," replied the woman.

"Where was the nearest fire station?"

"I already told you, we couldn't find an axe."

"Damn it, woman," yelled Dolan. "Where's the nearest bloody fire station?"

Pointing to the rising stream of water, she replied, "That way. Down the hall, make a right, then your first left."

"Would you hold my child please?" said Dolan as he thrust Kathleen into the woman's arms. He sat on the floor and began unlacing his boots.

"What in God's name are you doing?" asked the woman.

"I'm going to make a quick trip through the water and I want to be able to put on dry socks and shoes." He stuffed his socks into his boots, then tied the laces together and hung them around his neck. The boots rested on his chest. Dolan knew he could wade through waist deep water and still keep them dry.

He took Kathleen from the woman and ran toward the water. His first step into it stole his breath from him. The water was so cold his feet felt as though they were burning. His toes curled and his arches seized in cramps. By the time he made his first turn, the water was up to his knees. Dolan struggled down the hall against the increasing pressure of the water. He took quick, short steps to protect against loosing his balance and tumbling with Kathleen into the frigid water.

Murphy was in a nearby cabin. He was dressed in the shabby clothing of an immigrant and waiting for Dolan. The water was up to his knees but the cold had no affect on him. He put his ear to the door and could hear Dolan coming his way. After Dolan passed, Murphy turned the doorknob to step into the hall. As he opened the door, he discovered the increased pressure the rising water was putting on the door. It slowly opened but once the water level rose another couple of feet only the strong would be able to open any doors. Murphy shuddered back his thought of all the unfortunate souls down in the lower decks who would fall tragic victims to such a fate as the ship sank.

Murphy watched Dolan from the back as he approached his next turn. As he made his left turn, Dolan saw Murphy out of the corner of his eye, he stopped and looked at Murphy. The distance was too far for Dolan to recognize Murphy. To Dolan, it was just another immigrant trying to save his neck.

"Hey, mate," yelled Dolan. "Hang around, wouldja? I might be needin' your help."

Murphy held up his hand to say he understood. Dolan, buoyed the thought of assistance, continued his mission. The water was now waist high and Dolan's testicles drew into his body so quickly and deeply he thought they'd never again descend. On the right wall was the fire station. He could see the empty case that once held an axe. All thoughts of the axe were pushed aside as Dolan saw what he was looking for. On a large spool was a fire hose. He doubted the entire length would reach the stairwell, but his plan didn't require the entire length, only a few sections.

In his haste to reach the hose, it didn't occur to Dolan where the broken glass would have landed. It was spread on the floor next to the hose. Dolan walked barefoot over the broken glass. His feet were so cold he couldn't feel the dozens of cuts the glass had made in the soles of his feet.

Tesla grimaced at the sight of the monitor. "Ouch! That's got to hurt. I remember once how a diode broke in my fingers. The cuts hurt like hell and I bled like a stuck pig."

"I don't think he feels a thing," said Marconi. "He's numb from the waist down and his adrenaline is surging. He's going to have to be part fireman and part acrobat to complete this next part."

"Did you ever hear the expression, I'd walk over broken glass for you?" asked Ellen.

Kathleen slowly nodded.

"Well, your father just did that for you."

Dolan began pulling the hose from the reel. The hose was in 50 foot lengths held together with shiny brass couplings. Careful to keep Kathleen out of the frigid water, Dolan pulled out two sections of hose. Keeping Kathleen in the crook of his arm, he quickly uncoupled the hose and began dragging it back toward the locked gate. The going was slow because of the weight of the hose in the waist deep water. Dolan called out the man he had left between him and the stairway. There was no answer to his shouts. He yelled out again disappointed and angry the man would abandon him while he was trying to help others.

He turned the corner and saw Murphy hadn't totally abandoned him. He was retreating against the flow of the water.

"Hey, Bucko," Dolan yelled. "I could really use some help!"

Murphy still at a safe distance to avoid recognition held out his hands in a pleading gesture. He could see Dolan struggling with the baby and the hose. From the pained expression on Dolan's face, it was clear to Murphy he was almost at the point of exhaustion. At the moment, there was nothing Murphy wanted to do more than run down the hall to Dolan and assist him, but he knew he couldn't. He did a quick about face and took off down the hall leaving Dolan to fend for himself.

As soon as Murphy was out of sight, he dropped to his knees and held his palms up toward the ceiling. "Dear Father Almighty," he yelled. "Please, let me help that poor man. It's breaking my heart to see him struggle so gallantly."

In answer to his request, the hallway light closest to him exploded in a shower of sparks and broken glass. Murphy knew his request was denied. He crossed himself and rose to his feet wondering where he should go next. He knew Dolan would somehow find a way through the locked gate. Murphy quickly transformed from his peasant clothing into a splendid, black tuxedo. He looked as fine as any of the wealthy first class male passengers. Had anyone rounded the corner at that moment, they would have seen Murphy vanish into thin air.

"Nice job Murphy," muttered Morse. Turning to Marconi he added, "He'll fit right in up in the first class sections. Dolan would have to be right next to him to recognize him."

"I've been thinking," said Marconi. "So what if he does recognize him? Would it really make a difference?"

Morse thought for a moment, and then replied, "I honestly think it would. All Dolan's got going is his own ability to save his daughter. If he uncovered our little miracle and then was told, 'You're right. I'm an angel, but I'm not helping you,' I think the effect would be devastating. He may decide to give up right then and there."

"I can see your point," said Marconi. "You're right. Murphy's going to have to keep his identity a secret for as long as possible."

When Dolan returned to the stairwell, the water level was mid-calf but he knew he had to hurry. Most of the group had departed, leaving the others at the gate. They had headed away from the oncoming water and ran towards the stern. Of the original group, all that remained were two couples. Dolan handed Kathleen to one of the women as he pulled the hose toward him with both hands. When he got to the end he ran it up the stairs. As his feet came into contact with the still dry upper risers, they left smeared, bloody footprints.

"Good Lord, man!" said one of the men. "Your feet have been cut to ribbons. Let me have a look at them!"

Dolan looked at the amount of blood he was leaving and knew his feet didn't have minor cuts. He sat down on one of the steps and let the man take a look at the soles of his feet.

"You've got several nasty gashes on each of your soles! How did that happen?" asked the man.

"I was barefoot," said Dolan. "I didn't want my shoes to get soaked so I took them off. The glass was on the floor under the water. I couldn't see it."

"I can see a few pieces of glass. I'll pull them out!"

Dolan quickly nodded his head.

"It may hurt like hell, friend."

"Not bloody, likely," said Dolan. "My feet have been freezing cold since I stepped into the water.

The man took out a pocket knife and unhinged the blade. Cradling Dolan's feet in his free hand, he deftly pried out the pieces of glass embedded in Dolan's feet.

"There ya go, mate," he said. "I think that's going to help a lot. With the glass out of your feet, the bleedin' might even stop."

Dolan clapped the man on the side of the arm. "Thanks, mate. Now help me with the hose will ya?

"Whatcha got in mind?"

"We're gonna tie one end to the gate and you and I are gonna pull the bleedin' thing off."

The men threaded the heavy canvas hose through the gate and secured it with a large bowtie knot. They put a large loop in the remaining end to act as a harness. The loop stretched halfway down the stairwell, giving them enough leeway to generate pulling power.

The men stepped into the loop and faced the gate. They decided to walk backwards to generate maximum force.

"Pull, matey," yelled Dolan. "Pull with all your might."

The men backed down the stairs and the hose became taut.

"Keep pulling," yelled Dolan. "It's working!"

The gate gave an audible metallic groan as pressure was put on it. Before the men could react, the gate snapped open and the men lost their balance falling backwards down the stairs. They both landed on their bottoms, but were saved from jarring injury by the standing water. The men let out whoops of delight as they saw they had access to C Deck and first class. They all doubted they would encounter any more gates. The men quickly scrambled to their feet and removed the hose harness. Dolan quickly reclaimed Kathleen and together they all scrambled up the stairwell.

CHAPTER XV

WITH THE EXCEPTION of an occasional steward scurrying by, C Deck was empty. Dolan knew they should head to the main stairwell for quickest access to the lifeboat deck.

The group made their way down the hall when Dolan spotted an open linen closet. Thinking about his cut feet, he stopped and peered inside. On the shelves were stacks of linen sheets, pillow cases, and assorted sized towels.

"Hey, Mates," shouted Dolan. "I'm going to take a moment and tend to my feet. You keep going and Kathleen and I will meet you topside in a minute."

One of the men mulled Dolan's suggestion. "We kind of hate to leave you, mate."

Dolan placed a folded bath towel on the floor and placed Kathleen on it. Then he grabbed a pillow case and started tearing it into strips. "I'm just going to bandage my feet. I'll be right up. Save us a seat at the nearest lifeboat."

The man nodded and gave Dolan a quick wave. "Right-o, mate, we'll see you soon. Be quick about it. We can't be sure what's waitin' for us up top."

Dolan sat down next to Kathleen and smiled warmly at his daughter. "We're almost there, darlin'. Daddy just needs a few minutes to bandage up his cuts."

He wrapped the strips of linen around his feet and tucked in the loose ends knowing that tying them off would make knots that would make it impossible to put on his shoes. He stood up and discovered his first aid had worked well. "Not a bad job if I do say so myself," he muttered. He picked up Kathleen and decided the towel she was laying on would come in handy as an extra layer of protection against the cold, night air. He kissed the sleeping child on her forehead. As he did, he heard a scream.

Dolan jerked around in the direction of the scream. It was a female's and it made his blood run cold. It was a terrified scream full of fear, outrage and pain.

"My Lord, did you hear that?" asked Kathleen.

Ellen gently patted her hand and replied, "Yes, I did. So did your father. Look, he's going to investigate."

Dolan trotted down the hall and heard another scream. He thought of setting Kathleen down, but decided she would be safer remaining with him. He continued down the hall until he could hear the unmistakable sounds of a struggle. Whatever had caused the scream was around the corner. Dolan stopped, pressed himself against the wall and listened.

Morse, Marconi, and Tesla were all watching with great interest. "Whatever caused that girl to scream is right around the corner," said Marconi.

Morse demanded silence. "Be quiet," he hissed. "Look, he's about to make his move."

Dolan stepped around the corner and froze. What he saw filled him with outrage and pity. A young woman was on the floor, on her back with her dress hiked up to her waist. On top of her and trying to spread her legs was her attacker, his pants down to his knees. Assisting in the attack were two other men, from the look of their dress, immigrants from the steerage section.

The woman got a hand free and raked her nails across her assailant's face, drawing blood. Her attacker screamed in pain and slapped her viciously, demanding his assistants hold her hands. The other two grabbed her hands and pinned them to the floor under their boots.

While they watched their friend mount the helpless woman, they unbuttoned their trousers and began massaging themselves to erection, waiting for their turn.

"Those filthy bastards," hissed Tesla.

"Thank God, Dolan is there to break it up," said Marconi.

The phone rang and Morse picked it up. He listened intently to the voice on the other end then replaced the receiver. Without looking at Marconi, Morse said, "He says you're welcome."

Tesla and Marconi looked at each other, their eyes wide in disbelief. They had actually caught God's attention. They each swallowed hard and returned their attention to the screen.

Dolan sat Kathleen down out of sight from the commotion then ran to the attack. The two men pinning the girl's hands saw him coming and stepped away, their eyes wide with fear of the advancing Dolan.

With her hands free, the woman grabbed her attacker's head and pulled it to her mouth. She clamped her teeth onto his left ear and bit down so hard she almost severed it. The taste of blood filled her mouth. She spit the blood into his face then tried to bite his lower lip off.

"I thought I told you fools to hold her hands down," he screamed. "Now get a hold of her before I…"

Before he could finish his sentence, Dolan delivered a brutal kick between the man's exposed buttocks, catching him square in the testicles. The air rushed out of the man's lungs before he fell over in agony. From the fetal position, he saw his friends turn and run. He hauled himself to his feet and unsteadily limped away.

Dolan momentarily thought about giving chase but knew he couldn't leave baby Kathleen. His spirits were lifted as he saw a ship officer turn a corner down the hall, placing the attackers between himself and Dolan.

"Stop those men!" shouted Dolan. "They tried to rape this woman."

The officer looked him directly in the eye and a shiver ran up Dolan's spine. The officer looked exactly like the waiter who had spoken to Dolan in the galley.

The officer stepped to the side of the hall as the attackers approached him. "Hey, you!" yelled Dolan. "Stop those bloody bastards before they get away!"

The officer stood by as the men ran past him. In all the confusion, Dolan knew he would have no chance of apprehending them.

"You scurvy son of a bitch," yelled Dolan. "I ought to wring your neck. You stood their like a frightened child and let them get away!"

Murphy endured Dolan's verbal lambasting, wanting to fire back that he could have stopped them with a snap of his fingers, but by doing so would have forfeited a miracle.

"You poor soul," muttered Murphy. "I want to help, but I can't."

"What did you say, you bloody yellow bastard?" yelled Dolan. "Did you say something to me?"

Rather than risk a confrontation with Dolan, Murphy turned and walked away.

"That's right," shouted Dolan. "Do what you do best, turn tail and run away. I better not see you again, buck-o, because if I do, I'll make you sorry your mother ever met your father."

Morse, Marconi and Tesla sat in silence. The angels were well aware of the unenviable position Murphy was in.

"That had to be hard for him," said Marconi.

"It's got to be killing the poor guy, not to be able to intervene," agreed Tesla.

"Sometimes it takes a lot of guts to obey orders," added Morse. "That kid is going to be an asset to us."

Dolan knelt beside the woman and instinctively pulled her dress down to its proper length. He helped her to her feet and attempted to give her a comforting hug. She pushed him away and turned away from him. When she did, her facial features became clear to all those who were watching the event.

"Oh, Dear Lord," whispered Kathleen. She grabbed Ellen's hand so hard the angel was surprised by her sudden burst of strength.

"What's the matter, dear?" asked Ellen.

"Did you see the woman they were attacking?" asked Kathleen.

"Yes I did," replied Ellen. "What about her, Kathleen?"

"She's my Aunt," whispered Kathleen.

"You're Aunt? But that would be impossible," said Ellen.

"That's my Aunt Colleen," replied Kathleen. "My Aunt Colleen raised me."

CHAPTER XVI

"HER AUNT?" SHOUTED Tesla. "Did I just hear her say that was her aunt?"

Marconi dropped his arms to his side and slumped in his chair. "This is getting better and better," he said. "I think she's mistaken about the woman being her aunt, though. I've gone through Kathleen Dolan's records a dozen times and there is no mention of an Aunt Colleen."

Morse accessed the databanks and researched the existence of the mystery lady. When he reached the proper file, he clicked the mouse and waited for the information to appear on the monitor. When it did, he scanned the information on the screen.

"Kathleen Dolan was raised by Colleen Quinn, nee Callahan," he said. "Colleen was a documented survivor of the Titanic disaster. But, she is absolutely no relation to Kathleen."

"Why would she think that was her aunt?" asked Tesla.

"Maybe it's because that's what she was told," said Marconi.

"What do you mean?"

"If this Colleen woman actually raised Kathleen, maybe she always let Kathleen believe she was her aunt. You know, to make her feel like part of the family."

"You've made an excellent point," said Morse. "These two women are soon going to be linked for the rest of their lives. Something beautiful is about to happen and we're going to have the privilege of witnessing it."

The men were interrupted by the buzz of a phone line. Morse answered the call and as he listened he broke into a smile. "That's a wonderful idea, sir. I'll take care of it immediately."

Morse hung up the phone then flipped a switch that Marconi and Tesla knew was rarely used.

"That was from the Big Guy," said Morse. "He wants us to take this to primary. He wants everyone to see this."

Marconi and Tesla knew what they were seeing was now being broadcast throughout Heaven. The event unfolding before them on the Titanic could now be witnessed by every soul in the Hereafter.

CHAPTER XVII

FOR A MOMENT, Colleen thought she was going to be sick. With hands on knees, she leaned over until she had her gorge under control. After a few deep breaths she stood up and faced Dolan.

"I want to thank you for your assistance, sir," she said. "Those filthy animals had me at their mercy."

"Or lack of mercy," said Dolan.

"Bloody right," said Colleen. "I swear if I ever see that scum again, I'll claw his eyes out!"

"I feel the same way about that cowardly officer," said Dolan.

"What officer?"

"He was just down the hall, watching the man run past him. He didn't lift a finger to help you. It was like he was ordered not to assist the passengers."

"Truer words were never spoken," muttered Morse.

"I know why I wasn't on the top deck," said Colleen. "But why aren't you?"

"They had us locked up like cattle below," said Dolan. "I guess they didn't want us shiftless steerage folks cluttering up the place. I had to fight my way up here with my…Oh my God, Kathleen."

Dolan ran down the hall and turned the corner. He found his daughter exactly where he had left her on the floor, wide awake and staring and a flickering light above her head. He scooped her up and lovingly kissed her, apologizing for having to leave her unattended. Holding Kathleen tightly to his chest, he returned to Colleen.

Colleen was amazed to see the baby. She instantly knew of the sacrifice Dolan had made to save her from her attackers. To assist her, he had to leave his infant daughter. The feeling of respect and admiration of Dolan was rapidly changing to awe.

"Did you guys see that look she just gave him?" asked Marconi.

"I sure did," replied Marconi. "It could have melted that darn iceberg."

"She looks like she just met the man of her dreams," said Marconi.

The room fell silent as Morse added, "It's a shame they've only got a very short time together."

Colleen gently pulled the blanket aside and gazed at Kathleen's face. "What an angel," she cooed. "And she's such a good little thing. She's not fussing a bit."

"That's because she's got a full belly," said Dolan. "She had milk a little while ago in the lower galley." Patting the bottle in his jacket pocket he said, "I've also got a spare supply for her later on the lifeboat."

"Which is where we better be headed," said Colleen. "By the way, my name is Colleen Callahan."

"My name is Dolan," he replied. "And this is my daughter Kathleen. Her mother died giving birth to her. We're on our way to America to start over."

"Unfortunately, we're not off to a very good start," said Colleen.

Taking her hand, Dolan said, "C'mon, we've got to get to the lifeboats." The newly formed trio walked briskly to the stairwell that would take them to the boat deck.

Murphy was helping load the remaining lifeboats. His job was to see that only women and children were allowed a seat. What was early indifference among the first class passengers was now full scale pandemonium. The great ship was going down fast by the bow and the decks were now at a steep incline. Anyone on deck had to plant their downward foot in order to maintain their balance. As Murphy helped a young mother and her two children into the lifeboat he scanned the hundreds of nearby passengers, looking for Dolan and baby Kathleen. Not seeing them, he looked at the lifeboat davits on the side of the ship and saw there were only 3, including the one he was manning, lifeboats remaining and were rapidly being loaded. The fact that he knew the baby would actually survive didn't ease his anxiety. Even in the freezing night air, Murphy had to continually wipe his brow to keep his stinging sweat out of his eyes.

Dolan, Colleen and Kathleen were scurrying down a hallway toward the first class gentlemen's lounge. Once through the salon they could exit out onto the promenade deck and the lifeboats for safety.

At the end of the hallway Dolan could see the door to the salon and the end of their challenging journey. Just as he was about to convey his thanks to God, the ship rumbled and shook dropping the trio to the floor.

Murphy felt the shudder and looked toward the direction of the disturbance. As he did, he heard the stays holding the ship's huge forward smoke stack snapping like taut yarn. As they snapped they let out a sound like a pluck of a guitar string. To his horror, he heard jagged stress cracks spreading across the enormous structure. The sound of bending, over-stressed metal filled the air as the smoke stack tumbled over, crushing everything underneath it. It hit the foredeck with a deafening crash then rolled off into the sea.

"What was that?" asked a shaken Colleen. "It sounds like the ship is falling to pieces."

"It probably is," replied Dolan as he helped her to her feet. "We'd better get to a lifeboat as soon as we can. I don't think this ship's got too much life left in her."

"It won't be much longer now," muttered Tesla. "Recorded history tells us she sinks at about 2:20 AM their time."

"What time is it now?" asked Marconi.

"Almost two o'clock," replied Morse.

Kathleen and Ellen sat in awed silence over what they just witnessed. Tears glistened in both of their eyes as they thought about the risk Dolan took to help a total stranger. Kathleen broke the silence and said, "What a wonderful man. Did you see what he did for Aunt Colleen? He may have risked his life to help her. Those thugs could have turned on him and beaten him to death."

"He's a very brave fellow," agreed Ellen. "He's quite a fine man."

"He certainly is," said Kathleen. "If there is a Heaven and I'm sure there is, I'll be looking forward to being reunited with him."

Ellen saw the joy in Kathleen's eyes and smiled warmly at her. Ellen turned away and her smile faded. That's going to be rather soon, dear, she thought.

Suddenly, the hologram before them began to shake and a loud rumble filled the room. Kathleen watched as her father, aunt and she, as an infant, stumbled in the hallway of the Titanic almost 100 years ago.

Kathleen stiffened in her chair. "What was that?" she said.

"I don't know," replied Ellen. "It sounded like some kind of explosion."

The ship was now at such a severe list, furniture began to shift in the first class gentlemen's lounge. Glasses still holding drinks slid off the tables and smashed on the floor. Wing-back chairs tumbled over backwards and the grand piano began to slide on its casters. It rolled across the lounge and crashed into the door Dolan was about to use to enter the lounge.

"The first class lounge is right behind this door," said Dolan. He outstretched his arm and walked into it to push it open. As his palm hit the panel he was knocked backwards by the resistance.

"What the devil is wrong now?" he said. He turned to Colleen and said, "Hold Kathleen, would you please?"

Colleen took the infant and watched as Dolan put his shoulder to the door. Although it still didn't open, they could tell at least it wasn't locked.

Dolan took a step back and surveyed the situation. "Something must have fallen against it," he said. "Maybe a sofa, or a lounge chair."

"Can we get through?" asked Colleen.

Dolan shrugged his shoulders. "I don't know," he said. "I put my entire weight into it and it barely moved. I don't think we have enough time to power our way through it. I think we'd better retrace our steps to a cross-over hallway and try to reach the lounge from the other side."

They turned around and froze. Slowly creeping up the hallway, advancing directly towards them was seawater. For the water level to be that high, Dolan knew that almost a third of the Titanic had to be under water.

Colleen turned to Dolan and with mounting panic said, "You've got to get us through that door!"

Dolan kissed the top of his right index finger and gently place it on Kathleen's lips. Her eyes tracked along his hand and up his arms until they met his. He smiled at his daughter and she bubbled at him, totally unaware of the danger they were in.

He quickly crossed himself and threw himself at the door with such force that a panel cracked. As he pushed with all his might, Colleen saw light appear between the edge of the door and its frame. Dolan was slowly, but surely, moving whatever was blocking the door.

"Keep pushing," she said. "You're moving it."

Dolan dug his feet into the hall carpeting and pushed with his legs, his thigh muscles burning with the exertion. The door continued to open as the piano was forced away. Dolan now had enough room to slide his upper body between the door and its frame. He braced his back against the frame and continued to push. The door opened a little more, allowing Dolan to place his feet against the door allowing his legs to take most of the strain. With his back firmly against the frame, Dolan carefully "walked" the door until the soles of his feet were on the door at waist level. The weight of the piano was no match for the strength in Dolan's legs. As he pushed, the door opened enough to allow Colleen and Kathleen to crawl under Dolan and through the door.

Through clenched teeth, Dolan said, "I'm going to need your help. Set the baby down and take my arm. On the count of three I'm going to let this door go. You'll have a split second to pull me out of the way."

Colleen nodded in understanding and carefully placed Kathleen on an out of the way easy chair. Returning to Dolan she grabbed his arm and planted her feet, ready to pull with all her might.

Dolan began the countdown. "One…two…three!"

He let loose the pressure on the door and sprang to his right. As he did, Colleen pulled his arm so hard she sat down on the floor. Dolan landed awkwardly on top of her as the piano crashed back into the door. Dolan scrambled to his feet and helped her up. Looking at the piano he saw that a corner of it actually poked through the door. "Nobody's going to be getting through there," he said.

Colleen wasn't paying any attention to him. She was staring intently out the windows of the lounge. Through the windows she could see a flurry of activity on the promenade deck.

"By Golly, he did it," said Marconi. "That was a magnificent example of strength and determination. That Dolan is strong as a…"

Tesla and Morse noticed the break in Marconi's sentence.

"What's the matter?" asked Tesla.

"They just lost the wireless. Don't ask me how, but I just felt it."

"If anyone could, it would be you," said Morse.

CHAPTER XVIII

IT WAS PANDEMONIUM on the boat deck. The forecastle deck was now awash and would soon be under water. All the thoughts that the Titanic was unsinkable were replaced by immeasurable feelings of dread. Every person on deck knew the ship was going under, it was only a question of when. Desperate men were offering bribes to officers for seats in non-existent lifeboats while others were trying to lash together deck chairs in an attempt to construct crude rafts.

Dolan, Colleen and Kathleen burst out on the boat deck and surveyed the scene. Dolan quickly saw all the lifeboats on their side had been boarded. He handed Kathleen to Colleen and bulled his way through a crowd of men gathered by the railings saying their final good-byes to their wives and children. As he reached the railing, he heard an over-head whoosh and looked up to see a stream of smoke and sparks snaking into the dark sky. It was a rocket fired as a distress signal to ships that would never see it. It exploded in a bright white light, and then slowly settled into the sea.

Dolan peered over the railing and saw a lifeboat being lowered. Its position between decks told him he had missed getting Colleen and Kathleen a seat by only a few minutes.

"I've got a woman and child here," he yelled to a crewman feeding a line through a davit. "Can you bring back that boat?"

The crewman barely acknowledged Dolan's presence. "Not bloody likely, mate," he said. "It don't work that way. Once we start lowerin', that's it."

From the top of the davit to the gunwale of the lifeboat, Dolan estimated the distance to be about 20 feet, not too great a distance for a climb down the line to safety. He scanned the area for someone in charge. Seeing an officer, he pushed his way through the crowd in an attempt to reach him. Dolan had an idea and wanted the officer's permission to implement it.

The officer was busy trying to keep a frantic crowd of doomed men from jumping into the freezing water and didn't see Dolan approaching.

Dolan reached the officer and shook him by the shoulders. The officer turned around and his eyes locked with Dolan's. Dolan's stomach tightened in a knot as certainty hit him as forcefully as the collapsed smoke stack had hit the sea. The officer on the deck was the same one who had ignored his plea for help when Colleen was being attacked. Up close, Dolan also recognized him as the steward at the locked gate, the waiter in the galley, the passenger who wouldn't help with the fire hose, and the peasant who befriended him those first moments outside their sleeping quarters.

For a moment, Dolan was no longer afraid. He had an instant feeling of warmth and peace. "Saints be praised," said Dolan. "It's you. Sweet Jesus, it's you. It's always been you."

Murphy knew his cover had been blown, but didn't want to risk the completion of the miracle. Mustering as much bravado as he could, he replied, "I don't know what you're talking about, sir. Now you'll have to excuse me, I've got lots of work to do."

"Hang in there, Murphy," said Morse.

"Dolan's onto him, you can tell by the look on his face," added Tesla.

Throughout Heaven the suspense was building. Everyone watching on the system wide monitors knew about Murphy and Mitchell's situation. All were pulling for Murphy's continued success. Many had their hands folded in prayer or were on their knees offering prayers to God.

The noise on deck was incredibly loud. Dolan knew the only way Murphy could hear him was by actually lowering his voice.

"I don't know who you are," he said in a deep, calm tone. "But I've got a pretty good idea what you are."

Murphy pretended not to have heard, but Dolan could tell by the change in Murphy's expression, he had heard him.

"I've got a woman and child here, will you help me get them into a boat?"

"I can't do that, sir," replied Murphy.

"You can't, or you won't?"

Murphy pondered the weight of Dolan's question. The wrong reply could have grave consequences on the miracle. Not wanting to destroy Dolan's fighting spirit, Murphy said, "I can't, I think by now you know that." Murphy closed his eyes and waited for the retribution.

"Oh, boy," said Tesla. "He's walking on thin ice."

Marconi realized he'd been holding his breath. He let it out in a rush and looked to Morse. "Did he step over the line?" he asked.

Morse shrugged his shoulders. "We'll soon find out."

After several seconds Murphy opened his eyes and saw he was still on the Titanic. He was positive he'd be allowed to continue. If punishment from above was going to occur, it would have happened by now.

Murphy looked past Dolan and suddenly had an idea. "Don't give up, mate," he said to Dolan. "Just because I can't help you, doesn't mean help can't be found. Sometimes it's right behind you."

Dolan turned around and saw what Murphy was gazing at. On the wall behind him was a life ring attached to a long length of coiled rope.

"Are you crackers?" shouted Dolan. "I can't lower them into the sea. That water is freezing."

"Who said anything about the water," replied Murphy.

"Way to go Murphy!" yelled Marconi. "Good thinking."

"Ingenious," added Morse. "That was a suggestion that any intelligent man could make. There was no Divine Intervention at all."

Dolan got Murphy's message. He ran to the railings and estimated the distance from the deck to the boat to now be about 30 feet. He grabbed the ring and the rope and raced to Colleen. He put the ring over her head and held Kathleen as she pulled her arms through the hole. Colleen didn't need to be told what was about to happen. Dolan was going to lower the baby and her to the descending lifeboat. With the ring now around her waist, she held out her arms for the baby.

""Not this time," said Dolan. "You're going to need all your strength to maneuver yourself into that boat."

Panic hit Colleen like a fist to the jaw. She stared wide eyed at Dolan. "You daffy fool," she screamed. "What about the baby?"

"You won't be able to help her until you get into the boat," explained Dolan. "Once you're there, I'll find some way to get her to you."

"But that means….you'll have to…" Colleen stammered and couldn't finish her sentence.

"That I won't be able to go," said Dolan. "I've known that for quite some time."

"I'll love her as though she's my own," promised Colleen. "I swear to God I will."

Morse, Marconi, and Tesla all felt their throats tighten. "She certainly kept that promise," said Marconi. Tesla and Morse swallowed painfully and nodded in agreement.

Ellen felt as though her heart was breaking. Although she knew it was coming, she wasn't prepared to witness Dolan's selfless act of love. She wondered what effect the hologram was having on Kathleen. She stole a glance at her and saw she was absolutely beaming. Kathleen looked at Ellen and said warmly, "He sure did love me, didn't he?"

Ellen gently squeezed Kathleen's hand. "With all his heart, dear," she said.

Dolan knew every second Colleen spent on the deck of the Titanic decreased her odds of a successful descent to safety. He paid out about 45 feet of lifeline and looped several feet of the excess around his waist to use himself as a human capstan. He would carefully feed out the line as Colleen repelled down the side of the liner.

"I'll never be able to thank you," said Dolan.

"You don't have to," replied Colleen. She ran to Dolan and aware he was holding Kathleen, carefully placed her arms around him. She pulled him close and gently kissed his cheek. "God be with you," she whispered in his ear.

They ended their embrace and Colleen went to the railing. She hiked up her dress and threw her leg over the rail. "I'll leave the rest to you," she said. "Don't let me down. I expect to be holding baby Kathleen before the lifeboat hits the water."

"You will, Colleen. I swear it. Now off you go."

Dolan watched as Colleen finished climbing over the railing. He braced himself for the tremendous pull he was about to feel.

"Here now!" screamed a low ranking officer. "Just what the bloody hell do you think you're doing? Get back on this ship immediately!" He ran to Colleen and tried to pull her back over the railing. With one hand, Dolan grabbed the back of the officer's jacket and pulled him away. The officer spun around to face the man who would dare interrupt his duty. "Listen here, you filthy bilge rat! You put your hands on me again, and I'll send your miserable soul up to Saint Peter!"

Dolan smirked at the officer's overblown threat and motioned with a cock of his head for the man to step aside. "You can give it your best shot later, bucko. I'll even give you the first swing. But right now I'm kind of busy and if you don't stay out of my way, you're gonna find out how cold that water down there is."

The officer muttered a curse at Dolan and stalked away. Dolan nodded his head to Colleen and she began her dissent. With Kathleen in one arm he played out the line with his free hand. It wasn't long before Colleen's feet left solid purchase and she was dangling in space between the decks. Passengers on the deck beneath Dolan were shocked to see a pair of legs dangling in the air before them. As they watched in disbelief, Colleen was lowered into full view. Once they realized what was happening, the startled passengers rushed to her assistance. Two men grabbed her by the legs and steadied her. Two other men grabbed the rope suspending her. The relief of the strain on Dolan was so great he was afraid Colleen must have fallen into the water. He quickly pulled in the slack and looked over the railing. He whistled sharply and the men assisting Colleen craned their necks to look at Dolan.

"Thanks for the help, mates," he yelled. "The little lady has got to get to the boat!"

One of the men yelled up to Dolan, "Not to worry, mate. She's in good hands. We'll help you get her on the boat." Looking at Colleen he said, "What do you say, Miss? You ready to continue?"

Colleen nodded her head in approval.

"Very well, Miss!" said the man. "Down you go."

With the help of the men from the deck below, Colleen was easily lowered into the lifeboat. As soon as her toes touched the gunwale, she was grabbed by the officer on the boat and disengaged from her lifeline. Once she was free, she was helped onto a seat by several of the lady passengers who alternated between blessing her for her rescue and admonishing her for her life-risking endeavor.

Dolan looked down into the boat and saw Colleen had safely arrived. His relief was great. Not only for her safety, but also Kathleen could now be placed into her protective custody. As he gave her the okay signal, he felt the deck began to shake. The vibrations traveled from his feet all the way up his legs. He grabbed the railing for support as the vibrations ceased. Dolan hadn't known it, but the vibrations were caused by boilers breaking loose from their mountings and sliding toward the bow of the ship. In a few more minutes the angle would be so steep they would gather momentum and smash through the hull.

Dolan's next step was to shimmy down the guide lines and hand the baby over to Colleen. He knew that jumping onto the line would result in immediate retribution from the men that were being kept away. To further increase his dilemma, he heard the unmistakable sound of a pistol being fired and the warnings of a near frantic officer ordering the men to stand down or risk being shot.

Dolan knew his only chance was with Murphy. He searched the deck looking for him. At a time when ship's officers should have been obvious, Murphy was nowhere to be found. Dolan went back to the railing and looked down. The lifeboat for Kathleen was only a few feet from the water. In another minute or two, the boat would be in the water and released from the lines. If that happened Dolan would have to risk dropping the baby and hope that somebody in the boat had sure hands.

He quickly scanned the deck and still didn't see Murphy. Dolan was about to give up on ever seeing him again when he felt a tap on his shoulder. He spun around and was shocked to see he was face to face with Murphy.

Dolan's eyes widened in surprise. "Where in heaven's name did you come from?" he stammered. "You weren't here a second ago. It's like you appeared out of..." Dolan couldn't complete his sentence. The words he wanted to use snapped off like icicles on a garage eave. An awareness washed over him like a summer cloudburst. There was something special about the man in front of him, something extraordinary.

Murphy finished Dolan's sentence. "Thin air?"

Dolan swallowed hard and slowly nodded.

Murphy smiled and quickly changed the subject. "Move quickly," he said. "We haven't got much time." He pulled Dolan over to the front davit of Colleen's lifeboat. He reached over the railing to steady the guide line for Dolan. "Give me the child," said Murphy. "I'll give her right back to you as soon as you're in position."

Dolan handed Kathleen to Murphy and stepped onto the railing. He grasped the line and pulled himself off the ship. His action drew raucous shouts of disapproval from the stranded men on board. Murphy turned and faced the angry crowd.

"Settle down, gents. Settle down," he yelled. "He's going down to hand off his little girl. You won't deny her her chance of survival will you?"

"What makes you think he won't take a seat for himself?" yelled an angry man.

"Because he promised me he wouldn't," replied Murphy. "He gave me his word and I believe him."

"He'd promise you anything to save his bloody neck!" screamed another passenger.

"Not to worry, sir," said Murphy. "I've got a contingency plan if he breaks his promise."

"Bullshit!" yelled a man,

Murphy pulled a pistol out of his pocket and cocked the hammer. He pointed the pistol at the crowd and they immediately drew silent.

"If he tries to take a seat on the boat, I'll put a bullet in the back of his head."

"You couldn't hit the ground with your hat," snarled a man.

Murphy aimed the pistol at a light bulb on the forward mast and pulled the trigger. The muzzle flashed and the light bulb exploded in a shower of sparks.

Murphy faced the man who had challenged his marksmanship. "You were saying?"

Murphy turned his back to the group and handed the baby to Dolan. He held her in one arm as his other arm held him to the line. Using his feet for added purchase, he started to slide down the line.

"Don't forget, Patrick," said Murphy. "You do have to come back."

Dolan looked Murphy in the eye and a realization started growing. It was warm, serene, and comforting. In total chaos, in what was probably the last few minutes of his life, Dolan was astounded to discover he was at peace.

"It was my destiny, wasn't it?" whispered Dolan.

Murphy slowly nodded. He didn't smile but his eyes had a warm, soft shine. "It'll be your reward, Patrick," he said.

Dolan slid down the line until he had a foothold on the prow of the lifeboat. He stepped into the boat and handed Kathleen to Colleen.

Ellen let out a sigh of relief. She looked at Kathleen and said, "He did it. You're sitting here right now because of what we just saw."

Morse, Marconi, and Tesla all sat back in their chairs and beamed. Each man knew they had witnessed something amazing.

"What a job! That was some adventure," said Tesla.

"That Dolan is one hell of a guy. I'll have to look him up and shake his hand," added Marconi.

Tesla stood up and cracked his knuckles, the joints popping noisily. "Anybody want a cup of coffee?"

"Where are you going?" asked Marconi. "According to my watch, the Titanic still has 15 minutes left."

"I've already seen the end of the movie," said Tesla. "I already know what happens. Besides I don't think I can bear to watch."

"Maybe you're right," said Marconi.

"Excuse me, gentlemen," said Morse somberly. "But I think something extraordinary is about to happen."

With one hand still on the line, Dolan hugged Colleen with his free arm. She held baby Kathleen up so he could say his final goodbye. He showered his daughter with kisses and promises of eternal love and guidance.

To everyone watching the holographic images, the scene was heartbreaking. Each person was silently wondering what they would do in a similar situation, while simultaneously praying they would never have to find out.

Dolan gave a last good-bye to baby Kathleen and shimmied back up the rope. When he reached the boat deck he hauled himself over the railing and stood face to face with Murphy.

Murphy was about to congratulate Dolan on a job well done when built up air pressure inside the sinking bow started blowing off hatch covers. The noise was explosive. Dolan and Murphy could see the covers spinning into the night sky, illuminated by the moon and the still blazing ship lights.

"It won't be much longer," muttered Dolan.

"I'm afraid that's so," replied Murphy. He sent out his hand for Dolan to shake, "You did a remarkable job," he said. "Your daughter owes her life to you. So does Colleen."

"You were there the whole time, weren't you?" said Dolan.

Murphy shrugged his shoulders as if to say, 'I guess so.'

"You were in the hallway outside my cabin. You were the steward, the waiter, even a ship's officer. It was always you."

Murphy sheepishly smiled and slowly nodded.

"I'm pretty sure of what you are. I figured you're not of this Earth, or at least not of my Earth," said Dolan.

"You're right, Patrick."

"Why?"

"It's kind of a long story. Perhaps you should spend your last few minutes preparing your soul."

"My soul is prepared," said Dolan. "If it wasn't, would you still be here?"

"You've made an excellent point."

"Just tell me why," pleaded Dolan.

Murphy paused for a moment then said, "Kathleen. It was her idea."

The ship lurched as the stern started to rise dramatically into the air. As it did, the lights suddenly went out.

"But, how?" said Dolan.

"It was a prayer. A prayer she made and that was answered ninety seven years from now."

"Oh, my dear God," whispered Dolan.

"That He is," replied Murphy.

A thought occurred to Dolan. "Look, angel...I'm sorry, but I don't even know your name."

"It's Kyle, Kyle Murphy."

"Look, Mr. Murphy, you could stop this couldn't you? You could stop it right now. Save all these people. Save the pain and suffering. You could do it with the snap of your fingers, couldn't you?"

"It's not allowed," said Murphy. "It's my order not to. These people are all going to die. You're going to die, even if I wanted to and tried to stop it from happening."

Dolan was beginning to overbalance. He had to grab onto the railing to remain steady. He looked down at the water and saw his daughter's lifeboat pull away. For the first time that terrible evening Dolan was afraid, not afraid of dying but afraid there was something he must be overlooking. A deafening crack of wooden decking and the ominous groan of strained metal made him jerk his head sternward. Pieces of wooden decking were flying into the air and several portholes burst in a shower of glass. It was obvious the weight of the stern was causing the doomed liner to split in two. He immediately knew he didn't have much time left. So did everyone else left on the Titanic. Faced with sure doom, the remaining passengers panicked as the bow settled lower into the freezing ocean. It was total pandemonium and Dolan had to scream to be heard. Face to face with Murphy he shouted, "My girl is safe because of a prayer, right?"

Murphy nodded.

"By any chance her dying prayer?"

Another nod.

"Well, what about me?" he shouted. "Will God grant me a dying prayer?"

"I can't speak for God, Patrick," replied Murphy. "But maybe if I knew what it was I could help out a little."

A sickening groan of tearing metal filled the air. The stern was about to separate from the bow. "Her memories," shouted Dolan. "If I had her memories I could die in peace. What a gift. What a gift indeed. Please, dear Father, hear the last prayer of your faithful servant, Patrick Dolan. Please hear my prayer!"

The deck they were standing on suddenly rocked. Dolan's feet went out from under him and he found himself in midair about to land on his back. Before he did, he saw Murphy disappear.

CHAPTER XIX

MORSE JUMPED TO his feet and ran to his telephone intending to make the phone call to God. Knowing what Murphy was planning to do, Morse was planning to place the request on Murphy's behalf.

Before he could reach the phone it rang. He picked it up and shouted into the receiver. "Get off the line! I need it cleared immediately, and that is an order."

Morse suddenly fell silent as his eyes opened in amazement. Tesla and Marconi both wondered what could have caused the sudden change in Morse. In a few seconds he had gone from frantic to serene.

As he listened to the voice on the other end, Morse's mouth fell open. He hung up the phone and slowly turned to his assistants.

"It was Him," he whispered. "He knew what was coming and said it was okay. Murphy doesn't need to ask for permission. He's already been given it."

Tesla and Marconi's mouths had gone dry, swallowing was now a chore. Neither one had expected the phone call from God.

"What does He want us to do?" rasped Tesla.

"The instant Murphy shows up, send him right back to that ship," whispered Morse.

"Where did he go?" said Kathleen. "Where did your friend go? He just disappeared."

Ellen was wondering the same thing. Surely Murphy wouldn't abandon Dolan in his time of need. Before she could speak, Murphy reappeared. He had left the Titanic and returned in the time it took Dolan to lose his footing and fall to the deck.

During Dolan's fall Murphy appeared in the hallway outside Morse's office. As soon as he did, the door burst open and out ran Tesla and Marconi. Murphy was startled by the wild look in their eyes.

Seeing Murphy, they both began screaming at him. "Back, go back!" shouted Tesla.

"You have it," yelled Marconi. "You have permission to grant the prayer. God Himself gave it to you. Please, get back to that ship!"

Murphy didn't need to be told twice. In a half of a heart beat, he was back on the Titanic helping Dolan to his feet.

It was now impossible to stand without hanging onto the railing. Hanging on with all his strength, Dolan had to shout to be heard above the pandemonium as the Titanic's stern became almost perpendicular to the ocean's surface. "For a second, I thought you'd left me and saved yourself!"

Murphy remained remarkably calm in the midst of the chaos. "I'm seeing this through with you, my friend. At the moment I need two things from you. I need you to trust me and obey me. Your gift depends on it."

Dolan's eyes widened in amazement. "My gift?"

Murphy nodded his head. "Saint Elmo arranged it with God. Your prayer will be answered. Now, I say to you for the last time, will you trust and obey me?"

At that moment the Titanic began to split in two. Dolan felt a lightness in his stomach as the stern started to fall back into the water. "I will," shouted Dolan. "In the name of Dear God in Heaven, I will."

Murphy gently touched Dolan on the forehead and said, "Let go, Patrick."

Dolan still clutched the railing in a death grip.

"Patrick, remember your promise. I said let go."

Dolan wrenched his eyes shut and let go of the railing, fully expecting to tumble away to certain death. It was the quiet that made him open his eyes. It was totally silent. The only sound he could hear was his own breathing. "Saints preserve me," he whispered. "Am I dead?"

Murphy slowly shook his head.

Dolan was amazed to discover he could easily keep his footing on the 45 degree slope of the deck. He had to stomp his foot on the wooden decking to make sure his feet were actually in contact.

He spent the next moment surveying his surroundings. What he saw had to be impossible. Time had come to a total standstill. The great ship was no longer sinking. Passengers were actually suspended in the air, caught in mid-jump between the Titanic and the frigid North Atlantic. He had to turn his head away as he saw a man stalled halfway into the ocean, his splash frozen around him, his arms spread out, eyes wide in terror and mouth open in an agonizing scream.

The lump in Dolan's throat was so painful his voice was reduced to a raspy croak. "Where are we?" he asked.

"On the Titanic," replied Murphy.

"My Titanic or God's Titanic?"

"For the moment, it's God's. Your Titanic just slipped under the waves."

"But how?" asked Dolan.

"We're in a parallel dimension to yours," explained Murphy. "You can't see it, but it's always there. Everything that happens in your dimension also happens here, only on a much slower time plane. This dimension's Titanic is also sinking only at a rate you can't experience.

It was necessary to do this so you could have your prayer answered."

"Am I dead in my own dimension?" asked Dolan.

"Not yet, but it won't be much longer. That's why we have to hurry."

CHAPTER XX

KATHLEEN WAS SUDDENLY confused by the events being presented to her in the hologram. Turning to Ellen she said, "I don't understand. It was strange enough to watch the past in my own apartment. And now I'm watching the past unfold in an alternate dimension to my own?"

Ellen understood her elderly friend's dilemma. "I can explain it to you, dear. We never expected your dad to have his own dying…" The words caught in Ellen's throat and she was immediately sorry for not being more careful. "I'm sorry Kathleen," she said softly. "What I meant to say was final prayer. We weren't expecting your dad to have a final prayer. Naturally, we're going to grant it, but in order to do so, we had to slow things way, way down. Keep watching, dear. If I know my bosses, I'm positive you'll be glad you did."

Marconi discovered he had been holding his breath because the sight before him was truly amazing. On the monitor he and Tesla were watching, the Titanic had just slipped beneath the surface leaving hundreds of passengers quickly freezing to death in the frigid water. Their agonizing shouts for help that would never come filling the darkness.

He resumed breathing and shifted his attention to the picture in a picture portion of the monitor and saw Murphy and Dolan at the railing of yet another Titanic.

"You're following all this?" asked Tesla. "An alternate dimension. What a great idea. I'm telling you, that Elmo is a genius."

Marconi and Tesla were not the only ones watching the miracle. If the residents in Heaven had their own version of Neilson Ratings, the event they were watching would have been the most widely seen program in history.

Murphy spoke quietly, yet firmly. "Over there is your daughter's lifeboat," he said. Dolan saw several lifeboats.

"Which one?" he asked.

Murphy waved his hand and accented the boat with a soft, lavender aura. "That one," he said.

Dolan fixed his gaze on the boat.

"Keep watching," said Murphy. "Don't take your eyes off that boat."

"I won't," whispered Dolan.

At that moment Dolan's peripheral vision began to fade. Shortly he was enveloped in total darkness with only the lavender glow in his field of vision. "What's happening to me?" he asked.

"It's your prayer," replied Murphy. "It's about to be answered."

The two men watched as a scene appeared in the soft light. It was a large steamer with several lifeboats approaching it. Dolan could tell by the position of the sun on the horizon that it was just past dawn. He could barely make out the ship's name on her side. "Carpathia? Is that ship named Carpathia?"

"Yes," replied Murphy. "The Carpathia went down in history as the ship to rescue the survivors of the Titanic disaster. One of whom is your daughter. Once she received the distress signal she immediately set out to Titanic's last known position. She was over four hours away and unfortunately, by the time she arrived there was nothing she could do for the passengers in the water."

"One of which is me," said Dolan. There was no sorrow or fear in his voice. Only the firm resolve of a man who knew he had to play the hand he was dealt.

"The Carpathia," whispered Kathleen. "What a beautiful sight that must have been. Look at their faces. Look at the joy of relief."

It was an amazing sight. Ellen's eyes welled and a tear ran down her cheek and fell into her lap.

"Can my father see this?" asked Kathleen.

"He's seeing the same thing we are," replied Ellen.

"Right now?"

"At this exact moment."

The scene in the lavender light faded and was replaced by the sight of a bundle being hoisted in a sling.

"Is that her?" asked Dolan.

"Is that me?" asked Kathleen at the sane time.

"It is," replied Murphy and Ellen in unison.

"Where's Colleen?" asked Dolan.

"She's still in the boat. She wasn't about to take her eyes off Kathleen for a second," answered Murphy.

Dolan was then treated to the sight of Colleen being pulled over the railing onto the deck. The moment her feet hit, she hurried over to the seaman who was holding baby Kathleen and carefully took her from him.

Another seaman wrapped a large blanket around her and the infant. "She hasn't had any milk for hours, please help her," wailed Colleen.

"Right away, Ma'am," replied a seaman who darted off to the galley to warm the child some milk.

Tesla slumped in his chair and smiled broadly.

"They made it," he said.

Marconi adjusted a setting and pushed a button on his console. "Fast forward to New York Harbor," he said.

A most unusual sight appeared in the respective hologram. It was the Statue of Liberty in the middle of the North Atlantic.

"She's truly beautiful," remarked Dolan.

"It's what they saw as the Carpathia passed her on the way to the pier," said Murphy.

The Statue of Liberty faded away and was replaced by an image of Kathleen being tucked into bed by Colleen. They shared a bed in a very small room in an obviously shabby apartment.

"For a while they had to live in a tenement," explained Murphy. "There was no other way. But Colleen always kept things neat and clean. To Kathleen it all seemed perfectly normal living in a crowded building wearing hand me downs."

"I remember that Teddy bear," said Kathleen. "He was my favorite thing in the world. I must have had him until I was six or seven years old."

"Eight," said Ellen.

For the first time since the hologram appeared, Dolan felt sad. "I was taking her to America for a better life," he said. "We could have had that in Ireland."

"Not to worry," said Murphy. "Things get better."

Marconi smiled and pushed the fast forward button. "Making things better," he said.

The next image was of Kathleen at the table blowing out the candles on what was obviously a birthday cake. Dolan counted the candles and saw that Kathleen was now 5 years old.

Dolan was taken aback by his beautiful little girl. "Oh my goodness," he whispered. "What a beauty she's become."

"Daddy's little girl," replied Murphy.

Back in the Brooklyn apartment Ellen marveled at the image she was seeing. "You were such a pretty child," she said to Kathleen.

Kathleen ran her fingertips over the wrinkled skin on her face. "Time certainly has a way of changing things, doesn't it? You certainly can't say the same thing about me now?"

"But my dear, you are beautiful," said Ellen. "God may change our appearances but He always keeps us beautiful."

While Murphy and Dolan were watching Kathleen lick frosting off her fingers, Murphy suddenly cocked his head and listened intently. "Okay," he said. Turning to Dolan he said, "We've got to speed things up a bit."

"Oh, please," begged Dolan. "Let me watch just a little longer."

Murphy was understanding but knew he had to be firm. "We're sort of on a schedule, Patrick. We've got to move on." With a sweep of his hand, Murphy changed the scene.

A family room appeared and in it was an enormous Christmas tree. Decorating it were Colleen, Kathleen and a gentleman who was very fond of Colleen. Although the room wasn't spectacular it was a far cry from the tenement conditions Dolan had just seen.

"What are we watching?" asked Dolan.

"Christmas, 1929," said Murphy. "The gentleman in the image is Colleen's husband, Kathleen's step-father."

The word step-father stung Dolan. Murphy sensed this and replied, "Don't let it bother you, Patrick. After all, Colleen was entitled to live her life, right?"

"You're right. I'm sorry."

"The stock market had just crashed but it didn't affect Kathleen's family much. He had a secure position as a middle manager with Consolidated Edison."

"What's a stock market?" asked Dolan. "Cattle?"

Murphy smiled. He had forgotten they were in 1912 and as an Irish immigrant, Dolan wouldn't have had much knowledge about the Dow Jones Industrial Average.

"Never mind," he said. "Keep watching,"

The scene shifted to the right. They were now look-ing across the room to a door. Kathleen went to the door and opened it. In stepped a young man who took her in his arms.

"That's her husband, William Thomas O'Hara," said Murphy.

"Her husband?" said Dolan. "He's no more than a boy."

"No more than you were," replied Murphy. "This is their first Christmas. They were married earlier in the year."

"God bless them," said Dolan.

"By the next Christmas, they'll have made you a grandfather for the first time."

"The first time? How many grandchildren will I have?"

"Six," replied Murphy. "Six beautiful grandchildren. They in turn produced 23 great grandchildren. All are alive and well and living in 2009."

"Did the great grand kids ever get to know my Kathleen?"

"Of course they did. Very well, in fact…" A sudden realization hit Murphy like a slap in the face. "Oh Dear Lord," he gasped.

Murphy's outburst scared Dolan. He began to search the area, but nothing had changed. "What? What is it?" he asked.

"You haven't known. Through all this you haven't known."

"Known what?"

Murphy had to make an attempt to calm himself down. He wanted to make sure he spoke clearly and slowly. He wanted Dolan to hear his words the first time. Things were progressing too quickly for him to have to repeat himself.

"From the moment the ship hit the iceberg, Kathleen has been watching you from the year 2009. She is alive and living in Brooklyn, New York. Another Angel is with her, helping assist in this miracle. Your daughter is approaching the end of her life's journey and she wanted to be able to somehow witness your incredible adventure of this morning. We heard her prayer and answered it."

Dolan had clung onto every word. Murphy had conveyed a message that touched his heart. "That would make her almost one hundred years old," he said.

"Ninety-seven to be exact," replied Murphy. "She's been watching your every step. She's watching you right now."

As incredible as the story sounded, Dolan believed every word. "If she can see me, why can't I see her?"

"The miracle wasn't set up that way," replied Murphy. "But maybe, and I mean maybe, there's something that could be done about that later. In the meantime, take a look into our hologram and wave to your daughter. After all, she has been waiting for a very long time."

Dolan turned to the light and held up his hand, gently flexed his fingertips and mouthed the words, I love you Kathleen."

It was utterly still in the operations center of Heaven. Tears collected in the nostrils of Morse, Tesla and Marconi. None of the men dared reach for a handkerchief and blow their nose as each thought it would be a sign of disrespect. For the moment, each man used the back of their hands to remove the tears.

Back in her apartment, Kathleen found herself in the happiest moment of her life. Her heart was soaring as she watched her long dead father waving to her and telling her he loved her. Even though she was sure he couldn't see her, she waved back and said, "Hi, Daddy. I love you too."

Murphy gently grabbed Dolan's wrist and pulled his hand down to his side. "I'm sorry, Patrick, but we just don't have the time."

"What's going to happen next?" asked Dolan.

"Keep your eyes on the hologram," advised Murphy. "Things are going to be happening rather quickly."

With the wave of his hand, images began to appear, only much quicker than before. Dolan saw quick scenes of life's milestones. He witnessed births, graduations, weddings and holidays. He saw changes in fashion, housing and technology. Kathleen's life and the life of her family flew by in rapid succession. The hologram spewed out kaleidoscopic images of color and light.

As the scene shifted in Kathleen's apartment, the light show was visible on the street below. To passersby, they all thought the resident of the apartment must be the proud owner of a state of the art, high definition television.

Suddenly the images began to slow down. Dolan didn't need to be told what that meant. The final scene was the funeral of Kathleen's husband, William O'Hara.

"He was a fine man, Patrick," said Murphy. "He was a devoted husband, a loving father and an adored grandfather. He was the love of Kathleen's life."

"I would have liked to have met him," said Dolan.

A broad smile crossed Dolan's face. "That's part of the magic of this night," he said.

Dolan couldn't understand what Murphy found so amazing . "What could possibly be so amazing at a time like this?"

"You've already met him," replied Murphy. "In fact, you were one of the first to greet him when he arrived in Heaven. Don't forget, my skeptical friend, you've been dead for almost one hundred years. All we're doing at the moment is repeating history."

As soon as the words left his mouth, Murphy cocked his head and listened to a message only he could hear. Turning to Dolan, he said. "I'm sorry, Patrick, but it's almost time. Take one last look."

As Dolan gazed into the hologram a new image began to shape. It was of two women. One was quite elderly and in an easy chair, the other, a woman much younger. The younger woman was tenderly holding the older woman's hands.

"Is that….?" The words caught in Dolan's throat.

"Yes, that's her," replied Murphy. The lady with her is my associate, Ellen Mitchell. She's been with Kathleen the entire time."

Dolan and Murphy watched as Ellen leaned over and whispered into Kathleen's ear. Kathleen nodded and with a quivering hand raised her fingertips to her lips, kissed them, then blew the kiss to her father.

"Thank you, Daddy," she whispered. "Thank you for giving me my life." Kathleen returned her hand to her lap and turned to Ellen. "I think it's time," she said softy.

"Don't be afraid, dear," said Ellen. "I'm going to stay with you."

"You've been so very..." but before she could say "kind" Kathleen O'Hara peacefully passed away.

Ellen kissed her on the forehead and shifted Kathleen's position in the chair so her hands could be lovingly placed into the sign of the cross.

Getting up from her chair, Ellen crossed the living room and turned on the television. When the police would come to investigate, their report would show that Kathleen O'Hara, of Brooklyn, New York, had died at home of natural causes, while watching her television.

Ellen placed an anonymous call to 911 stating she hadn't seen the elderly lady from Garfield Place in several days then quietly left the building not knowing if she would ever be returning to Brooklyn again.

"Did I just watch my daughter pass away?" asked Dolan.

"Unfortunately she did," replied Murphy. "But I'm hoping you won't be too sad. After all, she did live a rich, full life and thanks to Divine Intervention, she died extremely happy. You saw it for yourself."

"Sad is the last thing I'll be when I die," said Dolan. "My gift from Heaven is making my heart soar."

Murphy couldn't agree more. The smile on Dolan's face was radiant. It was a stunning display of love, gratitude and devotion.

"You don't have to convince me of that," said Murphy. "I can see it in your eyes."

"What's next for me?" asked Dolan.

Even though Murphy had been expecting the question, it still stung him. "I'm afraid it's over," he said gently.

His smile never faltering, Dolan said, "I'm ready."

"Take a deep breath, Patrick. You're going to want a lot of air in your lungs."

Dolan inhaled deeply and held his breath. As he did, Murphy gently placed his hand on Dolan's head.

The shock of the frigid water forced the air from Dolan's lungs. He was now in the water where the Titanic's stern had slipped into oblivion. His hands and feet became instantly numb as warming blood was retreating to protect major organs. In the middle of hundreds of bodies, Dolan and a few others were struggling to remain alive. Dolan swam over to a body bobbing on the surface, supported by a life ring. Seeing the man currently using it, no longer needed it, he slipped it off the man and took it for himself.

With the life ring supporting him, Dolan found he didn't have to exhaust himself by treading water. The numbness had now spread to his arms and legs. "It won't be long now," he muttered.

From behind him came a voice. "Don't be afraid, Patrick."

As quickly as he could, Dolan spun around until he was facing Murphy. He was astounded to see Murphy squatting down to be nearer, his shoes just inches off the surface of the water.

Dolan's teeth were chattering uncontrollably. Talking became difficult and his words were practically incoherent.

"I didn't…know if you'd…be coming back…or not," he mumbled.

"Patrick, this is breaking my heart," said Murphy. "Will you ever be able to forgive me for standing by and watching you die? I really need you to forgive me, Patrick. I really need to hear the words."

"You…you don't…need my forgiveness," muttered Dolan. "Why would I…ever need to…forgive you? I…I…I love you. You…you…you've given me…the greatest gift…a man could ever…ask for."

Dolan was tired, more tired than he had ever felt in his life. He knew he could end it by simply closing his eyes. Breaking into an enormous smile, Dolan said, "Thank you…dear friend. I'm off to be…with my Kathleen."

Murphy couldn't help but see how unusual and out of place Dolan looked. To anyone discovering his body, they would think he had seen God before he died.

I have to do something about this, though Murphy. I can't have Fifth Office Lowe coming upon him looking like this.

Murphy waved his hand in front of Dolan's face and it quickly changed from a look of serenity and joy to one of pain and anguish. When Lowe rowed by later that morning checking for survivors, he would see Patrick Dolan's face as a mask of suffering.

Back at Heaven's Command Center the mood was happy, but not raucous. There were no hand shakes, backslaps, or high fives among the men, just a contented feeling of a job well done.

Morse, Marconi and Tesla each felt as though they'd been up all night. They were surprised to see the adventure had taken only two hours and forty minutes.

"I don't know about you guys," said Morse. "But I need a cup of coffee."

"You and me both," replied Marconi.

"Who's buying?" said Tesla.

"You are," said Morse.

EPILOGUE

SAINT ELMO SAT at his desk with his sleeves rolled up and his collar button open. After the Dolan miracle he had placed a call to a very important colleague. It was one of the most pleasant calls of his distinguished and illustrious career. "That's right, Peter. O'Hara, Kathleen Dolan O'Hara. She'll be heading your way, momentarily. Please process her immediately and send her over to me. There's somebody I want her to meet. Thanks for the favor, Peter. If there's anything I can ever do for you, just let me know."

Elmo hung up the phone, waited for the line to clear then placed another call. "Connect me to Mr. Hoover, please. Edgar? This is Elmo. I'm fine thanks. I trust you tuned into the recent proceedings? It was wonderful, wasn't it? I was wondering if you would do me a small favor. Would you please send a man over for Patrick Dolan? Tell him his daughter is on her way to meet him."

LaVergne, TN USA
16 July 2010
189867LV00001B/1/P